FORCE

FORCE OF NATURE SERIES BOOK 6

KATHI S. BARTON

WCP

World Castle Publishing, LLC
Pensacola, Florida

Copyright © Kathi S. Barton 2013
ISBN: 9781939865601
First Edition World Castle Publishing, LLC July 3, 2013
http://www.worldcastlepublishing.com

Licensing Notes

Cover: Karen Fuller
Photos: Shutterstock
Editor: Eric R. Johnston

CHAPTER 1

Myles walked along the sand-covered beach and let the wind blow over him. He was content. Not unhappy or sad but simply content. He needed to go back home to Ohio, but for now he was simply going to enjoy himself.

He'd heard from Phil and the rest of them a few times over the past months, and not once did they suggest that he come home. Phil, his maker, had told him that he could come back when he wanted. He knew the man was serious, and Myles decided that he would do just as he'd said—return when he wanted to. Relax and enjoy himself before he had to return and become a working stiff like the rest of them. But the need to return was beating at him daily.

Myles felt useless there at home with all the Forces. He had his business of course, but he wanted more out of life. More of something that he just couldn't put his finger on. He knew that being bored this soon into his life as a vampire was dangerous, but he didn't know what else to do. And he knew that wanting so much now was going to be a problem, since he was bound to live for a very long time. Centuries, according to Phil.

The idea of living so long and seeing the world around him change was depressing. What more could happen to him? What else could come along that would wow him as much as he'd already seen in his human life?

Myles saw the woman jogging toward him. He'd seen her three times this week already and nodded at her in acknowledgement as he did every time he saw her. He'd never seen her this far down the beach before, but then he was out a couple of hours sooner than normal. He had thought that she lived further up the beach, but apparently he'd been wrong.

She was human and pretty, but not what he thought of as beautiful. He supposed her lifestyle had a lot to do with that. He knew that she did these runs to meet with her seller, and that by the time she ran, or staggered, back in the opposite direction he'd be on his way back too. At times he wondered if he should call someone and have her arrested or put out the word she was meeting someone. But he felt that he'd have to explain too much and he just couldn't make himself care any longer. Sometimes he hated his lack of caring.

The gulls were busy this morning and he walked around, giving them a wide berth. When he'd first moved into the beach house he thought to feed them the first few times he'd been out here, had even brought bread with him once to do so, but had seen a woman and her child nearly get bombarded by the winged creatures and had thrown his food away. No way was he going to be shit on by a fucking bird that seemed to have no regard for the person who held out crumbs for them. He was nearly to the pier again to turn when he looked back at the birds. Something about them looked odd.

There was a body up ahead. "Shit." Taking off at a run, he shooed the birds off the body lying face up in the sand. He looked strangely alive. The birds, scavengers, had done a number on his face and exposed skin, leaving almost nothing intact. He pulled out his cell phone and spoke rapid French in it and had the police coming to his location. They said that he was to wait right there.

He stood guard over the man, wanting to check for identification, but knew he'd leave some of himself on the body. He would bet his last dollar that he wouldn't have any on him anyway. The neat hole in the middle of his forehead was telling enough. When the first cruiser arrived Myles stepped back and let them do their work. Holly touched his mind a few minutes later.

"Are you having fun?" He told her he was having the time of his life. *"Liar. What are you doing that has you so stressed? I could feel it all the way where I am. Or have I interrupted a booty call?"*

"And where would that be?" She laughed and he knew she wasn't going to tell him. *"No, I'm not having sex, but thanks for thinking I would answer you if I was. I found a body on the beach near your home. He was being picked at by a horde of fucking birds when I found him. Male, late fifties, suit. He's been shot in the head, and his hands are tied in back."*

She was quiet, and he felt her move through his mind, looking at his memories. *"Might be Antonio Jesper. Looks a lot like him if it's not him. And good job on the age. He's fifty-three. Worked for a mob in the States until a few years ago. Got him into a little bit of trouble so he came looking for help. He'd turned in compelling evidence on his boss and disappeared. I'm assuming he has no ID."*

"I didn't check for identification but I've called in la police and they're here now. I called them as soon as I saw the bullet hole. I figured with enough people out this time of day

that some kid might have found him first. You think he was found and taken care of?"

"More than likely, he wasn't an overly bright man. He never knew when to stay put. I think he was moved several times in the little time he was supposed to be under their protection." He told her that they had found a gun on him when one of the cops pulled it from under his coat. *"That's odd. Usually they check for those before they tie them up. Especially mob hits. Maybe he was very cooperative and they forgot to check."*

It took him a few seconds of looking at the body before something occurred to him. *"He was tied up after he was dead. There are no ligature marks on his wrists and he doesn't have any bruises. And for the damage done to him from the birds, his suit is in remarkable shape. It looks pressed even though it's wet, and come to think of it, his hair is combed. This is really weird."*

"Humm, that is odd. Tell me, Myles, do you think it's really him or a person that looks a great deal like him. And tell me if you think he's really dead or making you want to think he is." She paused for a few seconds. *"Myles get out of there. I have a feeling that the shit is about to hit the fan and you might be in trouble."* He asked one of the French police if he could leave.

He made the young cop believe that he wasn't needed and that he could go without gathering the usual information like his name and address. He also decided to get something more from the "dead" man and made sure that he wasn't caught too. While he was bent over him he flicked his finger over his skin and drew blood. The blood flowed too freely for him to have been dead for long. Then he walked away as the confused cop told him he was free to go.

"I have a sample for you. I may have accidently drawn blood from a floater. Go figure. And I got away making sure everyone forgot me. Can you send someone to—Mother fuck don't do that." She was standing before him in a dark shirt and darker pants. He knew she was working when she put her gun in her holster and held out a vial for him. The woman was nothing if not prepared. He looked at her when she laughed.

"I was in the neighborhood and thought, what the hell, I'll go and see my good buddy, Myles. " She held the vial with the small drop of blood in it up to the waning sun. "Not much but should be plenty to figure out if this is our Jesper. Anything else you can tell me about our guy?"

"I don't think he's actually dead. But he's not a vamp. Nor wolf. I don't know what he is. I could be wrong about him not being dead. Might have been a fluke that I drew any blood at all."

She didn't believe him any more than he did. She looked at him, and he was tempted to look away. She was much too perceptive, and he didn't want her seeing what he was hiding. She didn't speak at first, but took his wrist into hers.

"You're not feeding." She ran her nail down his vein, which was sunken, and his skin was dry. "You have to drink blood once in a while because your body needs it. Have you fed yet?"

"No. And if possible, I never will again. I'll drink more blood, but I'm not going to bite anyone." He did look away then. "I don't mind being a vampire sometimes, and I'm happy every day that you and Phil saved my miserable life, but I'm not ready to do the whole vamp thing. I still have a lot of issues with it."

She bumped him with her hip. "I wished that I could help you with that. I really do. The only person I've bitten is Phil and he's—"

9

She stopped when he raised his hand. "That's part of the 'I fucking don't want to know' category we talked about. And I do not want to know that you bite him or where."

She laughed. "Okay. I'm going to take this in. You drink…and soon. I don't want to have to come back here and kick your ass."

After she was gone he went back to the house. He looked at the luggage sitting by the door. He supposed he could have told her he was leaving today and would be home soon, but he hadn't wanted to. Putting his gun and extra clip in the box that he was mailing home, he called the courier. It would more than likely be home when he got there. He hated being without his gun almost as much as he did his wallet.

Myles arrived in the States just over twenty-three hours later. He was exhausted and hungry. He went to the house he'd purchased before leaving on this long trip and found it full of food and several bags of blood. The top one had a note on it.

"I saw that you were leaving and wanted to give you a welcome home gift. The house has been cleaned too. What little there was to clean. Have you ever heard of a catalog to order furniture? Also you should really learn to throw things out before leaving a full fridge. Call us when you're rested. Love, H."

Taking one of the small bags out, he microwaved it for a few seconds and poured it in a glass. He didn't mind the taste, loved it actually and wondered why this wasn't the preferred method over biting anyone. It was a hell of a lot easier on his belly that was for sure. He shivered when he thought of his one and only time biting someone.

He drank a second glass while he made himself a sandwich. He knew that he should contact the Force family and let them know he was back, but he wanted to enjoy the quiet for a little while longer. He knew that Holly had told

Phil, but doubted that she would have shared with the others. She knew him better than he did himself, he thought.

The phone was ringing when he settled on the couch. He let it go to voicemail and thought again about getting rid of it. He had no use for a house phone and only kept it because he'd always had one growing up. When it signaled that he had mail, he closed his eyes and forgot about it. He woke with at start some time later.

"You really should learn to answer your fucking phone." Phil sat in the chair across from him, looking like he was staying for a while. "I need you to do something for me. It's about a case I'm working on."

"Can't I simply just rest? I have jetlag." Phil grinned. "Seriously. I'm not sleeping well, and I want to be here for a while. And you should really learn to knock. What if I had a girl in here? Did you ever think of that?"

"Yes I did and dismissed it. You'd have to bring her here, and you don't even have a proper bed. You remember before you left that woman who came up missing? We all thought she was dead and her husband finally confessed?" Myles nodded, knowing there was no hope for it. "Her sister has come up with something strange. She said she got a letter from her last week."

"The body was never found," Myles said. Phil nodded. "So? What does that have to do with the trial and case? He didn't kill her, so what. Mistake on the court's part. He's dead anyway, so who really cares? The man committed suicide if I remember correctly."

Phil handed him the letter. "She gave me a copy so I could gather clues from it. I did see a few things but not enough to lead me to believe that she's still alive. Well, except for a few lines. Now I want to see if you get the same information I got."

Myles yawned and took the letter. He was into the first paragraph when he looked up at Phil. He nodded and told him to finish it. When he got to the bottom, he saw the small drop of blood that she said was there. Handing it back to Phil, he sat back.

"This Chris Collier, do you think she's making this up?" Phil shrugged. "What do you want me to do? And if you tell me that you want me to chase down this sister, I'm going to fucking stake you."

"No. You can't. It's impossible for you to harm or kill your maker." Phil stood up and handed him a file with an evil grin. "There's all you need to find her. As you can see from the letter, the sister has told Chris that she's a creature of the night. Why she didn't just say vampire is beyond me. Anyway. I've made arrangements for you to see her tomorrow morning at her hotel. She is a smart-mouthed little thing, so girth up your loins. She will take a piece of you if she can."

Phil handed him the written information about the room number and hotel address and walked to the door. Before leaving, he turned back. Myles thought he wasn't going to like whatever he had to say and, when Phil looked around the house, he knew he wasn't. Phil was much too fussy about things not to comment on the state of his house.

"Buy some furniture and stop sitting around in an outdoor chair inside the house. You have the money to make this place a home, yet you sit in it as if it's a tomb. You do know that you're a young man, right? You have a nice place, take care of it." Myles flipped him off. "In your dreams, buddy, in your dreams."

After his tormentor left, Myles went to his office. His desk consisted of a large wire roll that he'd found on the back deck that had come with his house. And he had a chair. It was wobbly, but it worked for him. As well as anything else, he might need to run a small search and find what this thing for Phil was. The laptop that he'd had as a regular cop, then a detective, had served him well over the years. And so what if it took a little while to boot up and had to be talked dirty to once in a while. He booted up his computer and opened the file while he waited.

The first thing he saw was the copy of the letter that Phil had brought. He looked at the drop of blood and knew that someone, probably Holly, had had it analyzed. He saw the report on the third page.

It was ninety-nine percent of a match to the supposed dead woman. He had to look up her name. Millie Newman. And her death certificate was dated five months ago. About the time he'd left the area. He took out the picture of the new vamp.

Pretty in an old fashioned sort of way, he guessed. Her eyes were a nondescript brown, and her hair a mousy color. He wondered if the change to vampire had made her look much different and put the picture down, not really caring. There was the handwritten as well as the typed confession from her husband, Peter Newman, that he'd killed his wife in a fit of rage because she had been having an affair with the mail man. There was also a transcript of the trial. Myles picked that up and laughed. It had lasted for one day and had ended when the man on trial had died. He remembered being in the courtroom and thought he'd never forget it. It was by and far one of the most entertaining trials he'd been to.

When it had gone to trial Peter told the court as well as just about anyone else that would listen that his wife was having an affair with Dutch Crash. And that she had been having said affair for nearly ten years. And of course he'd known about it all along.

"And why did you not confront her about it before that night," the prosecuting attorney asked him when Peter, a man of doubtful educational background, had said again that he'd killed her. "If you knew for that long, why in a fit of rage, as you called it, did you finally kill your wife?"

"Because she gave me the clap." Everyone laughed and the judge threatened to toss them all out if they didn't come to order. He glared at the man in the witness chair and took several deep breaths before speaking.

"And in the future please call it by its rightful name, gonorrhea. 'The Clap' is not a term we're familiar with here. And have you been tested for this disease? Or are you guessing you have it?"

"Oh, I got it all right. Do you want me to prove it to you?" Peter started to unbuckle his belt, seemingly willing to prove the problem. The judge called the court adjourned until someone could control the man.

The trial had ended a day later when Peter had written out the confession and then had killed himself that night by chewing his wrist open and bleeding out. He wasn't found until the next morning. The whole thing had been put away as a solved crime. Of course, there had never been a body, but the confession was enough. And now this.

Myles spent the better part of the night on the files and the transcript. He read over the letter to Chris three times, wondering if there were really any clues. He picked it up again and read it out loud. He found all sorts of things simply wrong with it, but not really much in the way of clues.

"My dearest sister, I've been living in hiding for several months now and find that I can't live without you any longer. I know you've thought of me as dead all this time, and for that I'm truly sorry. But things have changed for me and, until now, I've not had the knowhow in contacting you. But I thought of a letter and knew that you'd understand.

"I have become something of a monster. A creature of the night no less. And, as such, I have been reduced to living in the shadows and darkness, seeing no one and speaking to few. I have been living in fear since the night Peter had me turned.

"I would love a visit from you. You would be safe with me as I cannot bring myself to think of biting you. I have a small place, but would welcome you into it. Say you will come.

"You may post me at the postal office here in Chicago. My box number is ninety-three. When you get to town, open the post and you'll find a letter addressed to you. I look forward to hearing from you posthaste. Love, your sister, Millie."

The letter was all wrong when he thought only of the wording. He knew it and supposed that Phil had as well. But the blood was true. Someone else could have written this or had her write it under duress, but Myles thought it was something else. Plus, there was no key. How was she supposed to pick up the mail if she didn't provide the means to open it? He made a note to ask the sister when he saw her.

He was glad that he was going to meet with the sister. He glanced up at his clock and realized he'd been sitting there most of the night and now only had a few hours before he went to see her. Stretching, he put everything he'd been given, as well as a few notes, into a file and got up.

Myles went up to his room. The vast room wasn't any more furnished than the rooms below. There was an air mattress on the floor as well as a rolled up sleeping bag. His clothes sat in laundry baskets around the room, and the one piece of luggage he'd brought from France was sitting opened on an empty cardboard box that his guns and ammo had come in that morning. He walked to the suitcase and pulled out his small toiletry bag.

After a long, hot shower, he dressed. He laughed when he thought of Phil's face when he'd first seen his selection of clothes. Even when Austin and Dallas, two of his best friends, had seen it, they had cringed. He walked to the closet and pulled out the first thing he touched.

Dark jeans hung on every hanger with a black or blue t-shirt right next to them. He had three pairs of shoes and three pairs of boots. He reached for the cleanest boots. He walked out of his house thirty minutes later, having drank another glass of blood.

Myles loved to drive and took his time getting there. He'd had a nice car when he'd been working, a company vehicle, but he'd purchased a nice little truck for hauling things. Not that he ever needed to haul anything, but in the event it came up he was prepared. He still had plenty of time when he pulled into the lot in front of the older hotel. He got out of his car and stopped. Someone was watching him.

He moved across the lot and reached for Connor. He knew he was close and told him what he was feeling. Myles paused at the door to let someone out and glanced around. He didn't know what he was looking for, so he simply went inside. He moved past the desk and to the elevator.

"I'm on my way," Connor told him through their link. *"I should be there in about five minutes. Also you should know that Holly is with me. She was having lunch with me at the burger joint down the street."* Myles told him he was headed up to the room.

He stepped off the elevator and made his way down the hall. The closer he got to her room he knew something was off. Myles pulled his gun. When he noticed that the door he was supposed to be going to was ajar, he let Connor know.

"Stay out. Holly and I are coming up now."

"I'll wa—" He was interrupted by a scream.

"Change of plans." He knew the moment he walked into the room that another vampire was there. He didn't see anyone

until a woman stepped out of the bathroom. There was another woman behind her. This one had a gun pointed to the first woman's head. She had a bloodied lip and a nice bruise on her chin. The vampire looked like she'd gone a few rounds with a champ and had come out on bottom. He put his gun away.

"You with her?" the woman with the gun asked. Myles shook his head. "You know her?"

Again he shook his head.

"I'm Myles Kramer. Phil Campbell was to have set up a time for us to meet this morning." She didn't move. "I'm a little early. Want me to wait in the hall until you're finished with whatever it is you're doing. Oh, and if she's selling Tupperware, I might have an order too."

He could see that the woman in front was a vampire from the way her body moved quickly and without any kind of hesitation. He could smell her as well and knew that she was not very old, but she was dangerous. When she hissed at him he felt his fangs drop, and he showed her his were much bigger, more dangerous. When she made her move, he was going to be ready. He knew without a doubt that he could take her because of Phil being his maker.

CHAPTER 2

Chris had been minding her own business watching the news and brushing her hair when her door flew open. The woman standing in her room looked at Chris as if she was a feast on Thanksgiving. She walked on her high heels as if she'd been born in them and she looked like she'd been done up by a pro. Not an eyelash out of place.

"You looking for someone?" Chris said snidely as she reached for her gun in the couch seat. She didn't pull it right away but held it in the palm of her hand.

"Are you Christina Collier?" the woman demanded. Chris didn't answer her. She knew that answering a question like that one could get you served by a processor or arrested. She wasn't in the mood for either one right now.

"Are you here for some other reason than pissing me off? Because if that was your plan, you did a bang-up job." The woman approached and Chris barely had enough time to fire the gun. The bullet entered her chest and knocked her down. She thought she killed her until she started to move. Christ. All she could think about now was how grateful she was for the silencer and the silver bullets she'd loaded in her gun the night before.

"You shot me," the woman said.

"Yeah, I did. Nice of you to notice."

Chris went to her and noticed her fangs. Fear curled in her belly, but she wasn't going to give in to it now.

She put the silver handcuffs on her and tried to ignore her screams. "We're going to start over," Chris said, "and you're going to tell me what you're doing in this room. My room, as a matter of fact, and one that I did not invite you into."

The woman kicked at her and tried to get away, but Chris, dragging her into the bathroom to knock the shit out of her or, at the very least, tie her to the heater she'd used earlier.

Now there was another fang face standing in front of her, ordering of all things Tupperware. Like he could use it.

"I would like for one person to be what they're supposed to be, you know?" She knocked the woman to her knees. "If I shot her in the head will she be dead?"

"Probably since that's silver in your gun. And a shot to the head is pretty permanent. I would shoot her heart though. It works much faster and no chance of a quick recovery." She didn't ask him how he knew about the ammo and nodded her thanks. "You might want to find out what she's doing here and why she had a partner downstairs."

The woman snarled at the man and jerked from her. She was glad now that she had a tight grip on her hair or she might have. Chris kicked her again. This was just supposed to be a meeting to ask about her sister, collect her if need be, and be on her way. She had better things to do than to drag vampires around her room.

"This is a little surreal for me." Then a wolf appeared in the doorway. No, make that two. Trying her best not to let go of the woman and run for the hills, Chris tried to make it seem as if this sort of thing happened to her daily.

"Come on in. There's still some of my breakfast left from earlier. If you promise not to eat me, I'll be more than happy to order us up a couple of steaks. You both want rare, I take it?" The man in front of her laughed. "You, I suppose, want what she's having. And not from me."

"No. I don't drink from humans. But I do appreciate your concern." He glanced at the two wolves. "They won't harm you. They're with me. This is Holly Campbell, Phil's mate, and this is my good friend and one of Holly's brothers, Connor. He's with the police department. You must be Chris Collier. And this would be... Felicia Key. She's been sent here to capture you, but not harm you. There is a man just outside the hotel. He needs to be taken care of too."

He was suddenly in front of her and touched his finger to her cheek. Every cell in her body screamed for her to step back and away from him, but she stood her ground. When his fingers came away bloodied, she watched as he put the droplets in his mouth and moaned. His eyes had darkened, and she found herself mesmerized by them.

"Someone is going to be very pissed at you, Myles Kramer. You should not touch what does not belong to you." After making her prediction, the female vampire jerked away from her, leaving Chris holding a handful of her hair. Before she could react and kill her, Myles was taking her to the floor and covering her with his body. She let out loud, piercing screams as she struggled, but after a few seconds, it was over.

"Open the curtains and get rid of her," Myles said, then looked down at the woman. "I'll take this. It's a tad dangerous to the rest of us."

Her gun slipped from her limp fingers. He stood up and held out his hand to help her. When she stood on her own, he laughed. Chris had no idea, but she thought she could get used to the sound of his laughter all day long.

"I would like for you to explain to me why you let her go. And where the hell did those..." She looked around for the wolves. "Where the hell did they go?"

"Holly is in the hall. Connor has gone to break the news to her cohort that she won't be coming down. Of course, in a few minutes he won't care either. As for the wolves, they left their clothing out there and have gone back to dress. And we didn't let her go, they killed her. But not to worry, no one will ever know." He moved to the bar and poured himself three fingers of bourbon and swallowed it down.

"I'm not paying for that. That shit isn't a part of the room." He poured three more fingers and downed it as well. Then he poured a second glass and handed it out to her. She walked by him and to the kitchenette area to wash off the blood on her face. He moved to the couch and sat down as a beautiful woman and a gorgeous man walked in.

"That was interesting. And the vamp should have not been able to withstand any light even the dim of this day. She was new, but not that new. She should have known you would have had her beat as soon as you walked in the room. Oh, I'm Holly, by the way. Have you been hurt?"

Chris dried her face and shook her head. "Who the fuck are you people?"

Then it hit her all at once. She dropped to the floor and tried to breath. She was growing light-headed, about to faint. Myles picked her up and sat her on the counter and shoved her head between her knees, not a dignified way to sit. Every time she tried to raise her head he would shove it back down.

"Do you fucking mind? I'm all right," she said. He still didn't let her up so she spoke from the most undignified position she had ever been in. "Are you really a vampire like her?"

"No. I'm what is considered a 'day walker.' A vampire with special abilities. My makers passed that on to me. And I'm not here to harm you as she was. She was to bring you to someone and not to hurt you. How did she get in here?"

"And those other two, are they wolves or have I lost my marbles? And for the record I didn't invite you in either, so how were either of you able to get in?" He laughed. "This is so not funny, you asshole."

"I'm not a normal vampire, as I've said. And you probably haven't unpacked your things yet, which does not make this your home. Next time, take a few shirts and put them in the drawers. And the wolves are as real as you and I." She mumbled that she wasn't so sure about that either, and he laughed again. "Some days, neither do I. If I let you up, will you promise not to faint again?"

Her head shot up so quickly that she nearly fell off the counter. Grabbing his shoulder to keep from falling, she glared at him. The man was really big. But no less annoying.

"I did not faint, you chauvinistic prick. I was slightly overwhelmed for a moment. You have some sharp-toothed bitch bang her way into your room only to be followed by Mr. and Mrs. Furry face and see what that does for your blood pressure." He helped her down, and she walked away. "Not to mention some stupid asshole who thinks I'm some weak-milked dumbass that doesn't know when she's fainted or not. This is my hotel room, and it's been like fucking Grand Central around here."

"I had an appointment, if you remember." He followed her to the sitting area. "I'm here to talk to you about your sister. And these two came to help you when I noticed that your door was open. So I ask again, how did she get in here, and how did you manage to get the drop on her?"

Chris sat down and looked around the room, just noticing that the drapes were open, as was the doors to the balcony. She wondered again what had happened to the woman. She looked at Holly.

"Will you tell me what happened to that bitch? She was in here before macho britches knocked me to the floor." Holly laughed and sat down beside Myles. Connor, the other man, started to close up the room.

"She won't be bothering you again. And Myles kept you from seeing why she won't be bothering you. Wolves are quite dangerous when they want to be. When we had her down, Connor cut off her head." She nodded to him. "Once the sunshine was able to hit her, she went up like smoke. Nice clean-up job when you can get it."

Chris looked around the room. Clean up job. She looked back at Myles and noticed that he was watching her very closely. Like he was waiting for her to lose it or something. She lifted her chin and glared. He was really pushing her buttons, and she was letting him.

"I'm perfectly fine," Chris said, to which Myles nodded but said nothing. "My sister? If you're a vampire like her, then tell me where she is."

"You do know that there is no network that lets all vampires know where all the others are, don't you?" She glared harder. "I will tell you this. The blood is hers, but the writing...did you think it sounded like her?"

"What do you mean?" She stiffened. "I just want to know where I can find her. The post office box number had a shit ton of mail in it, but she didn't come by to give me a key, nor did she send me one either. I thought it would come later, but when it didn't before I left, I figured she'd bring it to me or something."

"So the wording of the letter, that sounded like her too." He was asking her the same question that she had for her sister. Who? What? When? And where the fuck? "It was very old fashioned, and the prose was dating her to be much older than I would think she would be."

"She's older than me by ten years and I agree, but that's not my issue. My parents had me late in life. Millie will be thirty-six on her next birthday." She sat back on the couch. "You keep skipping around my questions. Where do you think she is?"

"I don't know. But I also think you're in danger." She snorted in response. "Is that a yes?"

"It's an 'I'm always in trouble' statement. What I do for a living puts me in places that girls my age usually avoid. Unless, of course, they're masochistic idiots. Which I suppose I am." She got up to pick at her breakfast, and Holly stood up.

"I have to go. Phil has been pissy since I came in here and he wants a full report from you later." She pointed at Myles, then turned to the other man. "Could you give me a lift to the house? I came here by other means."

Connor and Holly left, and Chris stood by the door once they were gone and looked at Myles. She was hoping he'd get the hint and leave, but apparently he was as stupid as he was handsome. His "thank you" startled her.

"The vampire that was here, had you ever seen her before?" She shook her head and pointed to the door. "I'm not leaving. When she came in, did she say your name, or did you tell it to her?"

Giving up, she closed the door and locked it, then went to her tray of food and began eating the rest of the cold meal.

"She asked me if I was Christina Collier. I didn't answer her, and when she attacked, I shot her."

He nodded and walked to the table where she was and took her last slice of bacon and ate it. "And then I showed up. She knew enough to know you were here but not what you looked like. So she wasn't sent by your sister, or at least your sister didn't tell her what you looked like. Did she mention her?"

"No. She just asked the question and when I didn't answer, she...you're a cop." He shrugged. "A vampire cop no less. How is that even possible? I would think that there are rules about blood suckers working with bloody pricks."

Laughing hard, he answered her. "No, I'm a private detective that was once a cop. Now I'm just helping out a friend. How did you know to contact Phil?"

He was good. She'd give him that. He was changing the subject to keep her on her toes and not answering what she really needed to know. Well, she'd been playing this game a lot longer.

"His name came up in a conversation once," she said. "I'm not really sure how now. I doubt that it matters now. How long you been a vampire?"

He grinned before answering. "Two years and counting. So you don't actually know him, Phil I mean. What makes you believe that your sister is a vampire? You've never seen a species like us before today, and I would bet never a werewolf either."

She shoved the plate away and saw the blood in her arm. Turning it over she noticed the long scratch that went from her elbow to wrist. He pulled her injured arm to him and sniffed.

"What the fuck are you doing? It's just a scratch." He pulled it back when she jerked it from him. "Let me go or so help me I will scream loud enough to bring every person is this hotel in this room."

"No you won't." He stood up and pulled her with him. "You need to get that sealed. And now. There are all sorts of nasties a person like her could have on her. But she put her venom in it, and you'll need to get it taken care of."

"Or what," she snapped, trying to get away from him. "I'll change into an asshole like you that sucks blood? I said it was fine. Let me go."

Her body was suddenly as close to his as they could get. Her hands pushed against his chest when he wrapped his arm around her waist. She could swear that she could feel his heart pound beneath her finger tips.

"If it doesn't kill you, it will make you very ill. You'll die if that was her plan. And I can't let that happen." She looked up at him, afraid. "Close your eyes and you won't get sick. Well, not as sick as some do."

She started to say something and he kissed her. Christ, it was like kissing during sex. His mouth was warm and dark tasting. When he cupped the back of her head, she lifted her arms up and wrapped them around his neck. She had the distinct feeling of movement, quick and light. When he lifted his head she felt dazed and dizzy.

"Hold on. You're going to be just fine." She staggered back from him and looked at the smirk on his face. Without thinking, she slammed her fist into his face and fell back again. She was falling, and there wasn't a damned thing she could do about it. She simply let the darkness take her.

~~~

Clint looked her over twice more at Myles's insistence. Her arm was still bleeding, but there was nothing that he was willingly going to do about it. He was already pissed off because he'd taken her blood at the hotel without thinking. Well, he had all his mental faculties now, and he wasn't taking any more of her in. He looked up at Austin when he came in.

"She's human?" Austin nodded toward Chris who was lying very still and pale on the bed. "And you brought her here because?"

"She's been scratched by a nasty vampire. The cut won't seal on its own, and she needs someone to take the poison out." Clint looked at him again before continuing to explain to Austin why she was here. "She's going to be very ill from this if someone doesn't clean it soon. And he won't help me."

"And for what reason do you believe Myles should do it?" Clint shrugged and looked at him with a smirk. Austin looked at him with a raised brow. "And the reason you don't think you should is what? You don't think she's worth it? You don't like the taste of blood? Tell me. Because right now all I can think of is the problems this is going to cause my pack having a human woman in my clinic."

Phil walked in at that moment and Myles leapt at him like a drowning man. "She's hurt and you need to fix it. Clint said it needs to be a vampire because it was a vamp that hurt her. You need to hurry because she's going to be sicker."

Phil walked to the woman and looked at her arm before putting it gently back on her stomach. He rumbled through Myles's mind quickly and without heed to how painful it might be to him. Phil sat down and glared at him.

"Then you should have done it. You know as well as I do that I can't." Austin cleared his throat, and Phil turned to him. "He's the only one that can do it. And I won't be responsible for her if you let her die. You have to do it, and you know why as well as I do."

Myles wanted to scream. These people knew entirely too much. He didn't want to help her either but someone needed to. He looked at Austin when he started to talk. Phil cut him off.

"She's his mate." Austin laughed, and Phil joined him. Myles wanted to drain the two of them and told them so.

"I don't want a mate. Not one like her. She's mouthy and full of questions. I like my quiet life and need it to stay that way. Besides, I'm not supposed to find my mate until I'm older, much older." He glared at the vampire. "You know, as old as rocks like you are."

"Well, then, I say lucky you, you've found her now." Phil stepped to her and looked at him. "If I do this, she will belong to me. Forever, even if you ever want to claim her in the future. She will be my child as you are."

When he lifted her arm, Myles felt the growl start to grow at the pit of his belly. When Phil sniffed the wound, Myles grabbed him around the neck without even realizing that he'd moved. Phil didn't struggle, and he didn't retaliate when he was put down either. Myles stepped back and fell to his knees. He'd done the worst kind of crime and threatened his maker.

"Do it. You know you must or I will. Or I'll let Austin have her. Either way, someone is going to save her."

Myles stood and lifted her arm up to look at the festering wound. It was getting worse. Even he could see that. He touched his tongue to her skin and moaned. He wanted her and he needed her. Looking up at Phil and Austin again, he spoke.

"I hate you both for this." Myles pressed his mouth along the seam of the cut. He sucked out all the poisons before he started at the top again and licked the wound closed. It wouldn't affect him because he was already vampire. His body could take that and much more. He took the glass of blood handed to him and drank. When he finished, he stared down at her. He could see that she was already getting better. He opened his wrist and pressed it to her mouth. She would need the extra blood of his to help her combat any of the poison that he might have missed.

"I don't know what to do with her." He glanced at them again. "And I don't care what happens to her."

After he pulled his wrist away and sealed the wounds, he looked back at her once and glared at the two men who were his friends. With a parting salute, he left the hospital and took himself to his house. He wasn't going to be made to do anything, and that was final.

But he had a feeling it was much too late for that.

CHAPTER 3

Chris woke sore and starving. She sat up in the bed and realized that she was in a sort of hospital. There were all the general things you'd find in one, but this one had more. There was a comforter over her as well as a view out the large picture window that took her breath away. She was still watching the deer playing when a nurse came in.

"Hello. Miss Collier, right?"

"Technically, yes, that's my name, but I would very much prefer that you called me Chris." Chris looked at her. "What are you doing anyway?"

"I have to take your blood pressure and temperature. As soon as I get that done, Susie will bring in your dinner."

Dinner sounded heavenly. She waited until she was finished before she asked where she was. The girl smiled, a dreamy look overcoming her features. Chris told her she didn't remember how she got here either.

"Oh, Mr. Kramer brought you in, and you're at the Force Compound Clinic. You should be able to talk to him if you'd like to call him." Chris wasn't sure who the Forces were, why she was at their compound, or who she was supposed to call. Myles or one of these Force people.

"I'd just like my stuff please. I have a major headache and I need to get back to my hotel." She wondered if she still had a room at the hotel and asked how long she'd been here.

"Two days. And I'm not sure you're allowed to leave just yet. I think Austin wanted to have a word with you." *Well, we'll just see about that.*

As soon as Susie brought in her tray, she almost walked away from it to search for her clothes. But hunger won out. She was devouring the last piece of roast beef when a large man walked in. Picking up the pie, she regarded him as she ate it with her fingers. He looked to be in a good mood. For whatever reason, that pissed her off.

"Are you the doctor?" He shook his head and sat down. "Well, whoever you are, I want my clothes. That other girl, the nurse, was very polite, but she said that some Austin person wanted to speak to me before I was allowed to leave. I leave when I fucking want."

"I'm Austin Force. And you're going to get a lot further with me if you don't think you can boss me around. I'm alpha around here and what I say goes." He was smiling, but she could tell he really thought she was going to listen. "And I'm not a pushover like Myles is."

"Whatever." She tossed the blanket off her and stood up. She was slightly light headed but made it to the small closet against the wall. She pulled out her things and started for what she thought was the bathroom and was stopped. The large black wolf sitting there startled her.

"That's my brother, Dallas. He's here in the event I might miss telling you something." Austin chuckled as he leaned back in the chair. "I would suggest that you cooperate."

She threw her bag at the wolf and, when he flinched out of the way, she slapped him on the nose. He yelped and jerked back from her. When he started back toward her, his powerful jaws snapping at her, she grabbed his front paw and jerked. He snarled, but she was closer to her goal. When a sudden shout had her leaping back and falling over, the wolf took her to the floor and wrapped his mouth at her throat. She didn't move.

"You're a stubborn little thing, aren't you?" The door opened and the wolf was suddenly gone. Before she could get out of the way of either the dark flash or the wolf, she was pulled up against a body, Austin's hard body, and he wasn't kidding around any longer. Everything stopped.

"Let her go." Myles was standing before her and Austin. "Let her go, or so help me I'll kill you both."

"You said yesterday that you didn't want her as your mate," Austin said. Chris was suddenly in Myles's arms. "When you told me she had to be protected, you said you weren't going to come near us, that you didn't want her. You fucking idiot. What did you want us to do, kill you?"

She watched the two men. There was something going on here that she was pretty sure was way over her head. When she struggled to get out of Myles's arms, he tightened his grip on her. She answered by bending his thumb back against his hand until he let her go.

"That fucking hurt. What the hell is wrong with you? I've never seen a woman with more violent tendencies than you."

"Oh, and you've been so sweet and kind to me." She grabbed up her bag again and went to the bathroom. "You are driving me nuts with your hot and cold treatment of me. I'm fucking sick of things that go bump in the night fucking bumping me all hours of the day and night."

They better be gone when I come out, or heads are going to fucking roll. She slammed the door shut and locked it. She had a fleeting thought that they would be able to break in without much effort but was beyond caring at this point and started to get dressed. Fucking assholes.

~~~

Myles looked at Austin. He didn't look to be too terribly mad, so he started to explain. He had felt something from her and had come without realizing it. When Austin stopped him, he sat down as was told.

"You took her blood. That's how you knew she was frightened." Myles nodded, then shook his head. "Which it is? You did or didn't take her blood."

"I took it. But she wasn't frightened. She was pissed but not frightened." He looked up when Dallas laughed. "She was beating you and Dallas, and you damned well know it. She's a nightmare and the most violent person I've ever met."

"I don't hurt females and she grabbed my sore leg. Plus she fights dirty," Dallas added, rubbing his nose. "I haven't been hit on my nose like that since I was a pup. And she did it like she'd been taught by mom. All she needed to complete the picture was a wooden spoon and a tapping foot."

Austin nodded to Dallas, and he left them. When Austin sat, he looked at him as if he were going to have a talk with one of his children. Myles wasn't in the mood for that, so he stood up.

"I came here because you pissed her off, not to get a lecture. If you'd done as I asked and taken her to your pack house, none of this would be necessary. She's in trouble and you're the only place she can hide out."

"What makes you think I'm in trouble?" He turned when she spoke behind him. "I asked you a question. Why do you think I'm in trouble? And better yet, why the hell do you think I'm going to go stay with him? To keep me safe?"

"You don't have a choice. That woman came here to get you for some reason, and until I figure it out—"

"Until *you* figure it out? What the fuck do you have to do with any of this? So far, all you've managed to do is bring me here and piss me off. If that was your goal, then bully for you. You've made it." She looked at Austin. "You said you were alpha? I read about that a little. What exactly does that mean?"

"It means I'm the boss of my domain. I have a pack, a group of wolves that depend on me to keep them safe and healthy." Austin leaned back in the chair. "He might be right about you needing protection. Someone wants a piece of you. And as beautiful as you are, I really don't think it's a sexual thing."

"Thanks and no thanks. I'm trying to find out if my sister is alive or dead, not hang out with a bunch of furry dogs with a mouth full of teeth." She sat on the bed and began pulling on her boots. "Why was I here? What is the cost of me having a mini-vacation here?"

"You're not leaving here without protection." She didn't even look at him. "Damn it, don't you understand? That woman was going to kill you. Or take you to someone who would. She was the minion, and the next time someone comes, they'll be stronger and so on until you're where they want you."

"So they could be taking me to my sister? Good. It sounds like a plan to me." She stood up and glared. "That means with your type of help you're keeping me from finding her. I want you to stay away from me. All of you."

Myles had no choice. She'd backed him into a corner. "You're my mate and I forbid you to leave here. You're not going out somewhere that'll get you killed."

Austin stood up laughing. "Yeah, that'll work. You haven't had a lot of interaction with the opposite sex, have you? She's going to do just what you told her not to do, aren't you?"

Instead of answering Austin, she brushed by them both and out the door. Austin stepped in front of Myles before he could go after her. She was getting away, and he was letting her.

Before Myles could push him out of the way, Austin shook his head. "She's not going anywhere. There are nine wolves in the main lobby, and one of them is CJ. If she gets by her, the girl can take whatever the vamps think they dish out to her." Austin glanced at the door, then back at him. "I would suggest that you claim her before she does get herself in over her head. You won't have any more control over her, but at least you'll know where she is."

"I'm not going to claim her. I told you before, there's no room in my life for a female of any kind." He walked out the door, then onto the lobby. Six of the wolves were laying in a crumbled bloodied mess on the floor, CJ was limping, and the other two were gone. Myles looked at Austin when he walked up behind him.

"I guess she's going to be fine," Myles said as he walked out the door after making sure none of the wolves needed his blood to heal. He was nearly to his house when he felt Phil contact him. This was going to be a long night.

As Phil paced Holly sat and watched him. Myles yawned for the fourth time and wondered if this was ever going to end. When Phil stopped and glared, he knew he'd heard him.

"She's your mate for fuck sake. I told you to take care of her. Don't you even care that she's out there doing who knows what to whom?" Myles looked away. "I'm speaking to you."

"How do I know that this wasn't all a ploy and you didn't just make me believe she's my mate? You have all kinds of powers that nobody knows about. How do I know this isn't some plan of yours to get me to bite someone, and then you'll say, 'oops, sorry, I made a mistake, you're not her mate after all, but good fucking job on biting her'?" Myles stood up and started pacing. "I was having a nice vacation and, all the sudden, there's a dead body not a hundred yards from your house. Then I come back, and in less than half a day, you've got me meeting up with this broad and helping her find her sister. And that note you gave me? Lame. You wrote that or had some other woman do it for you. From the wording, I'd say your mom lent a hand in writing it. It sort of sounds like her when I think about it."

"First off, I can't make you believe that she is your mate, even if I wanted to. Do you honestly think me that cruel? Secondly, the sister is real. And she is missing. Third, the dead man somehow plays into this." He looked at Holly. "Tell him what you found out."

"You were right in thinking it wasn't Jesper. His name is Oscar, Daniel Oscar. He was working as a manservant for one of the vamps and was staying near where you were. He was reported missing the day after you found him. In my opinion, he wasn't supposed to be found until later that day. But you took your walk earlier than you normally did." She handed him a picture. "That's the man you found on the beach. We believe he was going to be a plant that would keep you in France longer than you'd planned. According to my sources, the cop you talked into letting you go wasn't supposed to be there. A more powerful vamp was. The cop was murdered an hour later. I would say someone was pissed that he'd fucked up their plans and took it out on him."

Myles sat down. "Why? I mean aren't manservants supposed to die like their vamp is? Sort of blow away or something?" She was shaking her head. "Then I don't understand how you connected the dots back to Chris. Unless you're saying that I was right again and he wasn't dead like they wanted us to believe."

"He wasn't dead. He looked it because everyone was supposed to think he was by someone powerful enough to do it or one of the cops there at the scene. When you gave me that sample, I knew immediately that he wasn't dead, as you'd guessed. Blood and very long dead bodies don't mix. And when the cop turned up murdered, and then Oscar's body disappeared from the morgue, that's when I figured out the connection." She handed him another picture. "This man is who he worked for. No one knows where he is other than the fact that he's wanted on several fraud cases as well as extortion and a few other things. Few know he's a vamp, and no one seems to know his age. He is also the maker of the vamp Connor and I killed. His name, last we heard, is Roy Gates."

"But how does that bring me to here? How did anyone know that I was taking the case and that Phil was giving it over to me? I only found out when I got here." He looked at Phil and figured it out before anyone could tell him. "She knew. Chris knew, and the vamp who was following her knew. Christ, she took her blood somehow."

"Not necessarily. Chris has been keeping in contact with her boss. If she told him, it's a possibility that Keys overheard her telling him. Or..." Myles looked at him. "She has tasted her at some point."

Myles tried his best to think through what Phil was saying. If the dead vamp tasted her, then Chris would be connected to Gates. If that was so, not even the death of Keys would stop him from knowing her every move. He paced more.

"What kind of vamp is this guy? Bastard like you, or someone I can deal with?" Phil laughed before he answered him.

"I don't know, actually. He doesn't exactly run in my type of bastard circles. I've talked to my mom. She has connections still and is looking into if for me. I couldn't because, if I did it, then the council would be involved and there are bound to be questions." He sat down. "What about Chris? What are you going to do about her? Because, regardless of whether or not you want her, she's still out there and the target of someone big."

"Nothing." Phil nodded, but sat there. "What would you have me do? Bring her back here? Tie her up and hope she doesn't get lose and kill me? Because mate or not, she's pretty hard on a man."

"She can't. Kill you, I mean. And tying her up? Might be fun. You tasted her blood, didn't you?" Myles nodded, not liking this. "Then you are as doomed as she is. You will die without her and, without you, someone will kill her. You're at a standoff with her. Claim her and help her or leave her to whatever mess she gets herself into and hope that things turn out all right."

After they left Myles sat in his living room with the lights off. He'd only meant to scare her when he'd tasted her blood that day. It had never occurred to him that she was his mate until he'd tasted her. He couldn't let this go, and yet, he really wanted to. Closing his eyes, he reached for her. She was sleeping.

Moving into her mind he searched for something, anything that would help him get this finished, so he could figure out a way to keep her safe and out of his life. He figured that he'd only drink from the one human before and vowed never to do that again. And keeping to the bags wouldn't be a problem for him. But what he found in her mind made his cock jerk.

She was having an erotic dream. About him. He watched as a bystander as she tried to seduce him. He touched his mind

39

to hers and took over. He thought about going to her, willing himself to her but knew that if he were there, with her, he'd really take her. This way was safer for them both.

Before he could do all the things he wanted to her, she startled awake. He found himself holding his breath as fear replaced her dream. When she spoke, he stood ready to go to her. Then he moved to be with her, fear making him override his own caution. He stood in the shadows as she looked around the room.

"Who's there," she asked as he stood as still as he could in her bedroom. "I have a gun, and it's loaded with silver. I will shoot your mother fucking ass." She would too. She'd start firing blindly and hit him and kill him before he was able to ask her what woke her. He stepped forward and let her see him.

"It's me. Put that thing away before you hurt someone." The light flared on. And there she laid with a gun in her hand, naked, the sheet pooled at her waist. Myles might as well have let her shoot him for all the good it was going to do him to deny wanting her now.

"What the hell are you doing here? And how did you get in? Again, you weren't invited." She pulled the sheet up over her breasts. "From what I read, you people can't enter a room without permission."

"It doesn't work that way on hotel rooms. I told you to put something in the drawers to make it your own. You haven't even put your tooth brush or shampoo in the shower like I suggested. You'd have been better off making this place your home in the first place. None of us could enter." He cleared his throat. "Do you always sleep in the raw?"

"Not that it's any of your business, but yes. And where can someone get a set of these rules? There seems to be as much information on you as there are smut books." She shifted on the bed, and he could smell her arousal. "I want you to go into the other room and I'll get dressed."

He might have. He wanted to believe he would have, but her voice had turned husky. Her scent, soft before, perfumed the air around them both and called to him. He took two steps forward and started to unbutton his shirt. The gun in her hand wavered but didn't lower.

"Do you know what you are to me?" he asked. She shook her head. "Mate. Did the books you read about my kind, did they tell you what that meant?"

"Yes. Some said that the couple would be bonded forever. Others said... What are you doing?" She sat up straighter on the bed and scooted back from him. "I want you to go...you have to go away now."

"No." His shirt hit the floor, then he took off his belt. "I want you as much as you do me. I can smell you, your heat and arousal. It's like a song to me, singing for me to take you and make you mine."

"I don't know what you're talking about. You're nuts. If you get into this bed with me, I'll shoot you." She swallowed twice loudly when he took off his pants. "I'm not going to let you take me like this."

"How would you like for me to take you, Christina?" He stood near the bed and stroked his cock through his briefs. "Would you like for me to drink from your pussy? Fuck you from behind? Or would you like for me to take you from that bed and take you hard against the wall behind you?"

She looked at the wall and he had his answer. Jerking the sheet off her, he pulled her up and stood her in front of him. She was gloriously naked and simply the most beautiful creature he'd ever seen. Touching her nipple with his finger, she moaned and swayed toward him.

"I want you." He leaned down and took the pert tip into his mouth and nipped at her. Her moan this time had her wrapping her hands into his hair and holding him to her. Opening his mouth as wide as he could Myles suckled as much of her warm flesh into his mouth as he could. Reaching down to cup her ass, he lifted her up and around him and walked to the wall.

Taking her mouth, he lifted her higher until her breast was at his mouth. As he rocked her over him, his cock burning to be set free, he felt his fangs drop. The need to bite her was overwhelming. Scraping them across her breast, then up her throat all he could think about was making her his. He sank his teeth deep into her and drank. Terror rolled over him, and he dropped her to her feet and fled to the other side of the room. He stood watching her as both of them breathed hard.

"I can't. I can't bite you." He turned to grab his pants and pull them on. She stood there staring at him as he jerked on his shirt too.

"Get out of here. If I ever see you again, I will shoot you in the dick."

He nodded and disappeared.

CHAPTER 4

Chris had her things packed and was ready to go the next morning. Even if she was only moving to another hotel, she wasn't staying here any longer. The place really had become like a train station with anyone and everything coming and going like she had a revolving door in place of the regular door. She walked into the living room area and saw Phil sitting there. She wasn't even surprised.

"I'm going to unpack every fucking thing I have with me at the next place I go. None of you people will be able to enter unless I give you permission." She went to the kitchen area and started packing up her things in there. Mostly water bottles and cans of soup, but all hers.

"It will do you some good. But Myles will be able to enter now as will I. Holly and the other wolves aren't bound by that rule, as they are different than us. Oh, in the event your information is a little off, garlic doesn't work at all. Nor, I'm afraid to admit, does Holy Water. Are you leaving?" She didn't bother answering him. "You should know something about Myles. He's been hurt."

"Big fucking deal. Haven't we all." She finished with those items and went to retrieve her bags. "Don't you have to be asleep or something? I thought all you... You're his maker."

"Yes. Very good. And as such I have to step in once in a while to help him. With you, for instance. He's very upset with not just me this time, but with himself as well." Phil leaned against the door where she was trying to get through with her luggage. "He seems to think that you're pissed at him."

"Well, good to know that my pointing a gun at him had some effect. Would you mind either getting the fuck out of my way or helping me?" He grinned, and she didn't like that.

"So you need me to help you?" He picked up a case and looked at her. She nearly said no and tried to figure out what he was saying. She nodded and he dropped the suitcase and came toward her.

"With the suitcases. Nothing else." She moved back until the wall hit her. "I meant with the suitcases. Mother fuck. I want you to get away from me."

"Too late." It felt as if she were tumbling. Over and over until she was sick with it. Then nothing.

Chris woke to a darkened room. She had no idea where she was, but she was pretty sure that the damned vamp had something to do with it. When she tried to get up, she realized she was cuffed to something. Or, in this case, to someone. She jerked hard on the chain and slapped him in the shoulder.

"What the fuck is the meaning of this? You call that guy right now and tell him I want him to let me go." Myles rolled over and looked at her, confused. "And don't think I don't know you had something to do with this. He said he was your maker. You put him up to this didn't you?"

"Phil? What did you...how did I get here?" She snorted at his question, not believing him for a second. "We're in his house. This is my room when I stay here. How the hell did we get here…? Damn it all to hell. I'm going to hire a hit man and take his fucking meddling ass out."

"I want you to get us out of here. I don't want to be near you." She moved as far from him as she could and realized she was naked. Again. "Where the hell are my clothes? Shit. Are you naked as well?"

He rolled to his back and pulled off the sheet that had been covering them both. He was. Wonderfully so. She turned from him and looked around the room as her eyes adjusted to the darkness of it. There was no way this could be happening.

"He must have put us to sleep and brought us here to make us mate." She didn't say anything in response. "Are you hurt? He didn't hurt you did he?"

She was, but not by anything that Phil had done to her. She'd been rejected sexually again. Not just by this man, but others as well. She wasn't what men liked in a woman, and sex didn't really appeal to her anyway. Until Myles.

"I'm just peachy. How do you contact him and tell him that this isn't fucking funny anymore? He can't just keep me here." She started to stand and fell back against him when she'd forgotten they were tethered together. "I'm going to see if there are any clothes in that dresser. You either come with me or I'll drag you along behind me. I'm not spending a second more around you without any clothes."

He got up, and she realized that they had been cuffed so that they either faced one another to walk or the one behind had to wrap their arm around the other and walk behind them. She opted for the arm wrap until he was pressed against her. She was killing Phil when she saw him next time. She had no such problems about finding a hit man to take him out.

Myles didn't say anything as he stomped across the room behind her. She jerked open the first drawer only to find it empty. As were the next two. When she bent to open the last ones, Myles moaned, and she felt his hard cock at her backside. She stood so quickly that she caught him in the chin.

"You're dangerous," Myles said. Chris tried to put as much distance between as she could until he pulled her back to him. "Behave yourself and we can get through this. I want you too much to have you rubbing your ass all over me like this."

Turning quickly and getting all tangled up in him, she tried to slug him again. "You bastard. I was not trying to rub all over you. I was trying to put clothes between us so you wouldn't have to be soiled by me too."

He pulled her body flush to his as he looked down at her. "Who said that I felt soiled by you? Christ, woman, I would like nothing better than to press you against that dresser and bury myself so deep in you that I never want to come out again. Who said that to you? Not a man with any kind of sense, I can tell you that."

She tried to get away, but he was much stronger and held her still. "Let me go. I don't know what you're talking about. Men adore me when I let them touch me, and I don't want them touching me. You either."

The more she struggled the tighter he held her. Before she knew what he was doing, he turned them around and took them back to the bed. She tried to stop him, but she was under him before she could turn away. She realized that she wasn't really putting up much of a fight and tried to renew her efforts.

"Stop. If you keep this up I'm going to be inside of you before I get answers." She stilled and looked up at him. "Good. We're not going to get out of here until he thinks we've mated. I have no desire to mate with you and... Will you fucking be still?"

She tried to fight him off, but finally he pulled her hands above her head and held them there. It held her where he wanted her, but she realized about the same time he did that her breast was only inches from his mouth.

"Don't do this." She might have convinced him if she hadn't arched up toward his mouth. "Please."

His mouth lowered until his breath over her nipple had it tighten. She moved her legs in an effort to squeeze them together, but he shifted as well and she felt his cock between her thighs. His tongue lapped at her breast until she was squirming under him. When he suckled at her breast she laced her fingers into his and held on. Christ, he was going to make her come.

~~~

Myles couldn't resist her any longer. He knew that it was a battle he wasn't going to win and knew that Phil wouldn't let them out until he took her. At this moment he was thinking of giving the man anything he wanted because he had forced this issue. As every part of his mind screamed at him to stop, this was a trap, his body said shut the fuck up and take her. He moved slowly at her entrance and felt her soak his cock. He inched his way into her slowly, filling her before moving back and doing it again. He wanted more than anything to slam into her but knew that, with his size, he'd surely hurt her.

"Myles, please. I need you to come. Please. When you do, I can help myself." He lifted his head. "I've never come during sex. If you come, then I can come afterwards. Hurry please."

"You've never come doing sex?" She shook her head and begged him to hurry. "I can't do that to you now. I have to have you come with me. As much as I'd love to watch you masturbate, having you come with me is more enjoyable." He sat up slightly and brought her hand down to her belly. "I'm going to help you first, try to take the edge off for both of us. Then I'm going come with you."

"No. It won't work. I'm not any good at this part. Men don't...I can't make men come. There's something wrong with me."

Myles looked down at her body and wondered what the fuck was wrong with the men she had been with. He reached for Phil with his mind. He was the only way that he could make her see.

"You have to let me go. I have to...she thinks there's something wrong with her and she won't let me please her. And I...I need to."

"I can't do that, Myles. If you don't mate with her, she'll be killed and then you'll turn rogue. I love you too much for that to happen. Just do as I've asked of you and the two of will can thank me later."

"I'm going to take her. I swear to you, but not like this. Please. I swear to you I'm going to make her mine. I can't...Phil, I can't think of anything else beyond claiming her." He let him have the memory of her words. *"You have to let me make love to her without the cuffs."*

The cuffs fell away. Before she could say anything, he moved down and settled between her thighs. Her scent called to him, and before she could get away from him, he took her clit into his mouth and suckled her.

Her scream startled him, and he thought he'd bitten her, but when she curled her fingers into his hair, he flicked his tongue into her tunnel and drank deeply. He lifted her legs, putting them at his shoulders, widening her for him. He wanted all of her, and spreading her like this gave him a view that he'd never get enough of. Lifting his head, he looked at her.

"When you come, I'm going to drink from you." He slid his finger into her tight sheath. "I'm going to drink from you until I'm full, then I'm going to fuck you."

"I can't come this way. I've tried so many times. You have to believe me. I have...I have something wrong with me sexually." He thumbed her clit back and forth and watched her. "Myles, please. I need you to—"

"Come, Christina. Come now." Her body froze for several heartbeats. Then she screamed. Her release was hard, strong, and flooded his hand. Leaning down, he lapped at her cream over and over until she was coming again. Then again. He couldn't get enough of her.

When she went limp, he lifted his needy body and moved up her. Myles nipped at her dewy skin and licked the tiny hurt. When he took her mouth, he knew she could taste her on him. Her moan of approval made his cock jerk, and he felt a tiny stream of his cum drip from the tip. Adjusting himself, shifting around until his cock was where he needed to be, he moved his mouth to her throat. The same terror rolled over him, but she lifted his head by a gentle tug of his hair.

"Are you going to bite me?" Her voice was hoarse from screaming. "I want you to. I don't have any idea why, but the thought of you taking my blood has me wet with need again. Which, I might add, I thought would be impossible since I've come like three hundred times already." He grinned.

"I would think closer to four hundred, but I lost count." He moved into her, slowly watching her face for any pain. "You're so tight around me. I feel as if I've found my home."

When he was buried to his root in her, he moved slowly. Each stroke brought him closer to coming, and his balls tightened to his body. He knew that soon, very soon, he was going to come and he was afraid. Afraid of losing control and hurting her.

His fangs were burning again, and he wanted to bite. He tried to still the fear of sinking them into her, but the need to mark and to drink was overriding him again. Myles licked a

49

path down her throat to her pounding pulse and she moaned. He wasn't going to have a choice, he realized. But he couldn't do it.

Her body shifted under his. When she grabbed his ass and wrapped her ankles around his hips, he closed his eyes. His climax was close enough for him to—

Pain shot up his arm.

She had bitten him. He watched her drink from his wrist, suckle at him as she looked into his eyes. When she tightened around him in her own release, he came, and came hard. Dropping to her throat, he sank his fangs deep without thought, without any fear. Blood exploded in his mouth as her taste filled him. Drawing deeply from her vein, he slammed into her, hearing her scream around his wrist as she took him into her again and again until he was empty. Myles knew that she was the one, that no one could have made her anything to him but what she was, his mate.

Satisfied and sated he looked down at her. Her eyes were closed. His wrist was still in her hand, and she looked happy. He smiled. He hadn't hurt her. In fact, he thought he'd made her as relaxed as he'd ever seen her.

When she let his wrist fall to her side, he dropped down onto her. He pulled her over him as he rolled to his back. His heart was pounding hard and he grinned. He fell in love as he lifted her chin up and looked into her face. He was terrified more now than ever.

"I have a mate." He heard Phil laugh through their connection when he told him. *"You're a prick and a bastard but I guess I owe you one."*

"You're very welcome, my friend. You'll see that this was for the best. She will need you more, I think, than any of us could imagine." Phil paused before telling him what he knew. *"Gates is looking for her. I haven't found out why yet, but he*

won't stop. Mom said he's a sadist and he has been in trouble with the council before. They have had a warrant out for him for a decade and no one could capture him. As of now he's wanted dead or alive."

"He'll have to go through me to get her." Myles pulled her closer and held her to him. *"I can't...she let me bite her."*

"Well, of course, she did. She's not a stupid girl." Phil laughed. *"Holly said to tell you thanks. She said you'd be down there less than a day before you gave in. I said a week."*

He told his friend that he was glad he could be such entertainment for them. He looked around the room. This was going to have to do them for a while as his place wasn't nearly as secure. He asked Phil if he minded.

"No, of course not. I was going to suggest it as well. You should ask the girl what she does for a living, though. It seems you two have a great deal in common. She has quite the reputation." Myles realized he knew very little about her and said as much to Phil. *"You have plenty of time to get to know each other."*

Myles nodded and closed his eyes only to open them a short time later. He got up and checked the lock on the door and found it to be no longer locked. After locking it with the inside key pad, he laid back down. This room only had one entrance: a hidey hole exit that Phil had told him about months ago. It wasn't on the plans, and no one but Holly, Phil and him knew about it. He would tell Chris when she woke.

He didn't sleep right away. He did something that he knew he shouldn't, but he wanted to find out if there was any connection to her and Gates. Anything. He did find that while Chris didn't know for sure that Keys was in her room at the hotel, she had seen her shadow three different times. Interesting.

He also found that Millie wasn't her true sister but a step-sister. And that over the years her and Chris's relationship had gone downhill. Millie was constantly complaining about how she had nothing when Chris had it all. And Chris felt as if she had nothing at all. Then he came across the encounter that had made her think something was wrong with her sexually. Grinning, Myles decided he was going to find the prick and make him understand that he was a fool. Right before he killed him.

Covering them both up, Myles thought of his terror at biting. He wasn't sure he could do it again but loved tasting her. She stirred in his arms and looked up at him.

"There are a few things about me you should know." She yawned as she continued. "I'm a cop too. I work in homicide. I've been there for about four-and-a-half years. I'm really good at it too. And if at all possible I want to be a part of everything that goes on concerning this case. Because, as we both have figured out, it has become more than a solved case and a missing body."

"I agree. Something isn't quite right even if you don't factor in that she's a vampire too. And I worked homicide as well before being converted to a vampire. Gold shield as a matter of fact." He kissed her nose. "What else?"

"I'm not really Millie's sister. She's my step-sister. And for the record, I don't much care for her, but she is my sister. I honestly don't know if I would have bothered with her at all if not for the fact that I made a promise." She rolled to her back and he adjusted himself so that he could see her. "She's been trouble for a while. And this vampire thing...she's been looking for someone to change her for a few years now. I haven't a clue why other than she watched a few television shows and decided that it was the life she wanted. She's been hanging out at bars she'd heard that vampires go to for...what do you call it?"

"Feed. It's called feeding. Do you know which bars they were? Or the name of the last one she was at before she disappeared?" She shook her head. "If you remember where, I can have someone look into it for us."

"Myles, I go my own way. I know that you think this thing between us might mean something, but I can't let it change my life. I have to figure out what happened to her." He didn't say anything. "I'm going back to Virginia when I figure this out, and you aren't coming with me. I know that you have a life and a family here. I wouldn't dream of asking you to give that up. But I have a good job and a nice house there."

He pulled her into his arms and kept his mouth shut. He had a feeling that telling her now that he didn't want to go back to bagged blood might get him into trouble. He was closing his eyes when he felt Phil touch him again.

"Bagged blood won't work either, any longer. You're either going to have to work this out with her or, as I said, you die. I'm sorry, Myles."

Myles didn't think he was in the least bit.

CHAPTER 5

Roy watched the man in front of him pace. He hated pacers. They would use up so much energy doing it and came no closer to solving whatever they thought they needed to pace for. He started to tell him to stop, again, but held his tongue. He might as well tell him not to drink blood.

"You do know that if the council is involved you'll be considered a danger to your own kind and killed on site, my lord?" Roy nodded. "If you know this, why are we still looking for this person? She is going to be your downfall, I fear. And that is not what you have worked for."

Anger surged through him, but he caught it before it took control. Control was everything to him. And what he could not control, he simply destroyed.

"You know that I will not let a mere slip of a girl take me down to any level, for I am too large for that to happen. She will only be my 'downfall,' as you called it, if we are caught. I do not plan on getting caught. Do you?" Leon Bird shook his head. "Good. Then I would like for you to go back to the hotel and find her. She has simply moved to another room to hide from the newborn that I mistakenly thought I could trust and control. I am glad that she has been dealt with, but I wish I could have given her my kind of justice and not that of a human."

"The man, Phil Campbell, he is the one that the sister contacted as soon as she received the letter. He is reputed to be one of the strongest vampires ever born." Leon went on as if he had not a care in the world. "I've heard stories of his special powers. Some say that he can eat silver and have it not affect him. And his mate? She is a special wolf that can kill anything and has the powers that he has."

Roy stretched his neck and, only when he popped it twice, did Leon turn to him. He paled, signaling his beast had come forth. He did not even try to rein him in this time but let him take his body slowly, by degrees.

Leon scrambled back quickly, but not quickly enough. Roy picked him up by his skinny neck and held him several feet off the floor. He let him see the monster that he was. He stared deeply into his eyes and let him see what others feared most. Him and all that he was.

"Do you think that Campbell will be any sort of match to me? Do you think that once it is known what I am, what I have become, that the council won't bow down before me and worship me as Campbell will? I am vampire. I am the most powerful being ever born. I am a direct descendant to the first family. I will be made king of my kind or they will die."

He dropped him, hearing bone break and smelling blood. Roy ignored it. He would not sully his body with such weak blood as this…this thing. He looked to the woman forever standing near his chair and told her to bring him lunch.

Seconds later, a young girl, a child really, was brought to him. He looked down at her and knew that she'd been drugged.

So deeply that she had to be brought to him on a litter. He looked at the woman who stood back by his chair.

"I cannot drink that. What have you done to her? She isn't fit for anyone of my stature." The woman trembled so he looked to Leon, who had returned healed. "Well? What have you done?"

"She and the others, my lord, they kill themselves if we do not keep them as such. They have heard what you do to them and they have such fear that they kill each other and themselves. Nine have died last week." The woman dropped to her knees and cried. Still Leon continued. "They will not last if we did not do something to keep them safe from their own selves."

He looked at the drugged child, then back at the supine woman who still had not moved. "Then she will simply take her place. Come to me and know that I give you a great honor."

She didn't move. Roy thundered his command for her to come to him and she rose from her feet. When she was within a few feet of him, he smiled. She was going to die for her insolence, but he was going to take her blood first. When he reached for her, she stumbled and he felt the prick of something enter his chest. Terror ran through his body. She had found it. Found the only weapon capable of killing him. But he'd seen no marks on her, no tat that said she was the one.

Looking down, he could see that it was nothing more than a shard of glass. No doubt from a piece of his own household items. Before he could move to kill her for it, she fell away and toward the window.

"I would rather see myself dead than summit to you," the woman said. The glass she'd slammed in his chest had narrowly missed his heart. He had known such fear, such terror, when he felt it and was so profoundly relieved when he saw what it was that he let it override his usual caution and jerked it from his chest and roared at her. When he stood to go to her, to kill her, she also moved and flung herself out the window behind her. Not a sound was made as she fell three stories to her death. Roy looked at Leon.

"She has killed herself." Leon nodded with disbelief on his face. "That puts me into a sad position, does it not? She has left me without a sex toy. I will need you to find a replacement as soon as possible." He looked at the child on the gurney. "Rid me of these doped donors. I would have a fresh lot by morning."

Leon nodded. "Yes, my lord. I will do as you wish. And the children, you mean for me to take them back to the home?"

"No, you imbecile, I wish them dead. Now." Walking to the window, he looked out, knowing there were men already cleaning up the body. "I want that woman that I turned recently. What was her name?" He knew it as well as his own. How could one forget a child of theirs?

"Millicent Newman, sire. But she is still wild, sir. Her conversion did not go as planned, as you know." Roy knew. He'd done more than he should have for her, and now he was stuck with the bitch. "Would you like another?"

"No. I said her. If she does not please me I will simply end her meager existence. I want her bathed and brought to my bed chamber as soon as it can be arranged." Roy moved through his mansion, knowing that his orders would be carried out.

Who he really wanted was the sister, Christina Collier. He had seen faded, blurry images of her in Millicent's memories and wanted to tame her, control her. He wanted a challenge and he had a feeling that she was going to give it to him. And he had no doubt that he would not completely control her, but she would be fun for a long while. Plus, he wanted to fuck her.

Fuck her until neither of them could walk. He wanted to bury his cock into her pussy and fill her. Roy smiled. She was going to be his before long, and he couldn't wait.

He went to his bedchamber and stripped down and lay on his bed. He wanted to wait for Millicent, but found that he could not. Taking his cock in his hand, he stroked it, thinking about the beautiful woman. When he heard his door open, he looked up to see the woman being led in.

"Leave us," he ordered. Millicent licked her lips and he commanded her to come to him. "Suck me off and I will let you live another day. Do it well and I will give you what you need."

She started to strip off her clothes, but he stopped her. She nodded, never taking her eyes off his cock, and got up on the bed with him. When she wrapped her small hand around him, he closed his eyes again and thought of Christina. Her hand, her mouth was what he thought of when the whore between his legs pleasured him.

Her mouth engulfed his cock. Roy watched her take him, her enjoyment evident. Every time she swallowed him down her throat, he thought of Christina's tight pussy taking him. Wrapping his hands in her hair, he held her still while he fucked her. He moaned when he felt his balls coat in her salvia. Rolling over, he continued fucking her mouth, but he thought of nothing but coming in another.

He jerked his cock from her mouth and told her to stand leaned over the bed. He stood behind her and looked at her juices running down her legs and wondered if Christina would be so wet, smell more delicious for him. He took his cock in his hand and guided it to her pussy, soaking it with her juices before he opened her ass and slammed his cock deep into her ass.

Her screams excited him. Roy fucked her tight ass while her blood made his way slick and easier for him. The harder she tried to get away from him the harder he fucked her, pressing her body to his bed and trapping her there. Then when he began to come he pulled out and jettisoned all over her. His cum mixed with her blood drove him wild, and he took her again.

Jerking her up, he tilted her head and sank his fang deep into her vein. Blood hot with fear and excitement filled his mouth. Swallowing, he moaned and felt it fill his body with energy. His cock hardened again and she pulled away. But he simply pressed her down and pounded her ass again. Drinking from her hot liquid, he spilled himself in her again and again. When he was finished he sealed the wound at her throat and walked to his bathroom.

"You'll be gone when I return and, with you, the filth of our union. Tell Leon to make sure you are ready for me tomorrow night as well."

"Sir, I hurt. I bleed so ba—"

"Do I look to you as if I care? Be gone." He turned the water on as hot as it could go and stepped in, calling for his manservant. *"I'm finished with this one. Bring me another and make sure that they are tight in the ass. I want a male this time. One that will fight me when I take him."*

"Yes, sir." Smiling, Roy knew that his command would be carried out and wondered why he had kept Oscar around for so long when this one was so much better at following his every wish.

When he came out of the shower there was a man chained to his bed posts. He was large and his cock was flaccid. Roy walked to him and wrapped his hand around his thickening cock. Kissing his shoulder and watching the man flinch away made Roy's own cock seep.

"You might fight me, but you will love it." Roy dropped to his knees and took his cock into his mouth. Over and over he swallowed the man deep. His balls heavy and full, he cupped them in his hands and twisted hard. The man could not reach him but he could curse, which was what Roy wanted from his victims. As soon as he was no longer fighting him but fucking him and moaning, Roy commanded him to come. This was going to be a long and fun night.

~~~

Austin was sitting at his desk when there was a knock at his door. He looked up to see CJ and his mother standing there as the door swung open. He knew immediately that something had happened.

"The children. Where are they?" He came around the desk quickly, ready to go for them. But both women shook their head and he knew terror like he'd never had before.

"Our children are fine. Someone…there was…" CJ fell into his arms. "They just came out of the woods. They just came out and sat on the deck."

Austin stood and reached for his brothers, commanding each of them to come to him. He heard the questions but ignored them. Something had come out of the woods and he wasn't sure what yet. He moved through the house to the front, bracing himself for whatever was out there. He heard Connor say to wait because he was near. Dallas said that he and Stacy were almost there.

Swinging the door open fast, he nearly missed seeing what was there. Whatever his mind had thought, it wasn't the group of children sitting there. He looked back at his mate.

"We gave them blankets. They wouldn't come inside but they took the covers. Austin, some of them have been bitten, and all of them are starved." She moved out to the porch and the children moved away from her. "They're terrified of me. They are so afraid of all of us."

His brother and their mates flooded the yard. Each of them had shifted to help with his call to them. Those that could not shift stood armed and ready to do whatever he needed. Austin dropped to the deck, his legs too shaky to hold him up any longer. Holly came out of the woods just as Phil appeared at his side.

"Vampire. They've been with a vampire and until recently too." As Phil moved forward, the children started crying. "I need to figure out whom. I need only to touch them to see what they have been terrorized with."

"You'll wait." CJ took charge and looked at the group, their pack. "We need to gain their trust first. For all they know you might be their next tormentor. Let's get them somewhere warm and then try to get them fed. Come on men, get shifted and dressed. We have a lot of work to do."

Austin sat in his office an hour later. The children, over a dozen of them, had not moved anywhere. And the food that his mom and CJ had given them was still sitting in bowls on the deck around them. Austin looked at Phil.

"I can help them. All of them, if you would give me permission. I can't do anything, as you know, without your say-so, because this is your land. You know that I can. But in return they will give me what I need as well." Austin nodded. "Thank you. But I will need to put them into a deep sleep first. I fear that if I touched them now, they might well hurt themselves more trying to get away. Is that all right too?"

Austin had already spoken to CJ. She didn't want them harmed. Neither did he, but two of the younger ones were dying. Even he could sense that. He looked to Phil for help and answers.

"Do it. I know that this is asking a lot of you, but they need help, and without you helping them, they'll die." Phil stood. "Is Myles going to help you?"

"He's on his way. He's mated with the girl. She's going to be difficult for him, but I think he needs the challenge. She's as stubborn as someone else I know."

Austin smiled as he stood. "And she gets more stubborn every day. I swear that if one of our cubs is half as stubborn as her, I feel for their own mates."

"I was speaking of you." Phil laughed when Austin growled at him. "You thought I was talking about CJ? She's an amateur compared to you."

The children were huddled in a tight circle still on the deck. Some of them looked at them as if they were going to be hurt. Others looked at them with a blank vacant stare. Those children frightened him the most. Austin was going to kill the bastard who'd done this to them and hoped that it was sooner rather than later. When Myles arrived, the young woman was with him. She was invited into the house but declined.

"Who are they, do we know?" Austin shook his head. "I've seen this look before. It's like shell shock. They've seen more than most of us do in several lifetimes and have shut down. As much as I hate to say it, I've actually seen it in kids younger than these guys."

Then Chris was quiet as the children started to fall over. He could see her need to go to them and he was glad for that. He always worried that someone would find a mate that wouldn't want children or even like them. His mom walked up beside them both. She spoke quietly.

"Holly said that they'd have to put them asleep one at a time starting with the stronger ones. If they didn't, they would fight harder for the little ones as they fell away from them. Once they're all asleep, they'll take away their memories. This will be most difficult on Phil, I think. He has a child now and he can only be thinking of what may happen to his own."

"What happens to the memories?" When neither of them answered her, Chris looked back at the two men just understanding what was happening, and felt her heart break for them. "Myles and Phil keep them, don't they? So they trade off their ability to help them and get to keep whatever horror those little ones have seen. I'm not sure I could do something like that. I have enough shit up here now that would make a priest run."

"Phil has done it before and Myles only a few times. It's hard on them but it helps so many. Phil has nightmares, though he doesn't talk about them. But being his mate, I know. I want to help him but..." Holly smiled when she finished telling Chris about her mate. "You look like you've had a good night."

Austin laughed when Chris blushed. When she glared at him he could see a bit of what Phil was talking about. She was stubborn and he couldn't wait to see her top one of his wolves again. He moved back when she took a step toward him. He wasn't afraid of her, but didn't want to get into a pissing contest with her so close to the kids. He laughed when she told him she'd take him on later.

When the children were all asleep they each carried them into the house. There had been beds made up for all of them. His mom had suggested that keeping them all in the same room seemed the best bet. Before Myles and Phil began, each child was washed down and put into large shirts and other clothes donated by other pack members. Two hours after they'd been brought in, Myles and Phil began their work.

It took them seven hours to erase their memories. Some of the younger ones who had been touched by the man had been easier to help. But the older ones, the ones who had seen so much more, had taken a little longer. By morning both men were exhausted and starving, an aftereffect of what they had done. Austin offered both them and their mates a place to rest. He watched Myles and Chris walk away before looking at Phil.

"Will he be all right with her? I mean he might…I don't know, take too much. I don't want her hurt too."

"I'm more worried he won't take anything from her. You know that he hasn't bitten anyone but her since…" Phil looked at the stairs where they'd gone. "He'll have to take from her or she'll make him. I have a feeling the girl knows a great deal more about our kind than I first thought."

Austin had wondered the same thing. He didn't think she'd looked all that shocked when he'd seen her in the hospital. And Holly said that she'd not freaked out when she and Connor had shifted or about having a vampire in her room. He looked up the stairs too. Phil was right, the girl was just too calm to just now be introduced to what CJ had termed "freaky shit."

He went into the living room and sat down, wondering about the kids. Thirteen of them in all and the youngest couldn't have been more than a few years old and the oldest probably only about ten. All of them had been bitten and a few of them more than once. Myles had said that more than half of them had been sexually abused. But they wouldn't remember that now.

And now they knew who had dropped them off. Not his name but his face. Myles had said that the man had told them that they must never tell. Must never speak of this to anyone or he'd come back to get them. Austin wondered if he had meant it or if he only said it to frighten them. Either way, the kids had been saved by him.

After poking his head in the door Phil said that he was leaving. He said that one of them would check on the children in the morning. Austin stood up and walked with him to the door. He stopped him before he left.

"You know who did this to them, don't you? I don't mean the person who made sure we found them, but the person who hurt them." Phil nodded. "It was Roy Gates, wasn't it?"

"Yes. But without letting the authorities know what we did to the little ones no one can know but us. What we did, what I did today, is a forbidden act for my kind. Even as a part of the council there is no way that we'd be able to justify what we did. You know as well as well as I do that we'd be put to death."

Austin nodded. "You're right. No one but us can know. But that means that no one but us can take care of the information that we gathered from them either. And I don't know about you, but I'm fine with that as well. I wouldn't mind dealing out some justice of my own. Especially someone who would purposely try to destroy young lives like he tried to do with those children."

Phil nodded again and looked out among the trees. "I'm in. I'm sure that, after this, Myles will be as well. Gates has fucked with the wrong family.'

Austin watched Holly and him drive away. Yes, he had fucked with the wrong family. Gates was going to rue the day that he messed with the Force family. They were a force all their own.

CHAPTER 6

Myles was exhausted and Chris knew it. She could feel it like she'd been wearing his body and now it was all her own. She followed him up the stairs and walked into the bedroom and waited until he sat down before speaking.

"You and Phil, you probably saved those kids' years of therapy." He grunted and she sat down on the chair near the fireplace and waited. "Why don't you lie down? I'll be really quiet until you go to sleep."

"No. You can't. Stay I mean." Myles looked frustrated as he continued. "I told you this morning that we can't do that again. I can't bite you like that. What if I had hurt you?" She watched him and knew something else. He was hungry. Very much so and he wasn't thinking of a cheeseburger and fries either.

"You're not going to feed from me, are you? Even though we both know that's what you need?" He looked at her sharply, and she felt his anger at her saying anything. "Well, what do you need from me? I've never done this before except with you. And that was during sex. I'm reasonably sure you're not horny. So what do I do?"

"You leave. Now. I'm going to be all right once I get some rest. It took a great deal out of me and I just need to rest." She nodded. She moved to the door, deciding to take the matter into her own hand and went back down stairs. But she needed help first.

She saw the cook in the kitchen. She looked at her oddly, but said nothing. Finally she asked how she could call Mr. Campbell. She needed to speak to him. CJ walked in just as she was asking.

"Something wrong?" Chris sat down and then stood up to pace and CJ looked worried as she asked her next question. "Chris, did Myles hurt you?"

"No. Christ no. But I might hurt him. I need to talk to his maker, that Phil guy. Can I use the phone?" CJ smiled and told her the number. When Phil answered she launched into her question. "He's hungry. And I'm pretty sure that ordering him an extra large all the way isn't going to cut it. And he's practically thrown me out of the room. Do I...I don't know...cut open an artery to make him do...what the fuck. This is by far the stupidest conversation that I've ever had. Feed. Do I have to cut something off to make him feed?"

His laughter made her feel better. "Nothing so drastic. You could offer yourself to him. See if he wants to feed from you."

"Nope. Turned me down flat. Said he needed a nap. I'd like to shove a nap up his ass. I can feel he's a tad on the tired side, but his hunger feels like mine."

Phil seemed to be enjoying her for whatever reason. She waited while he seemed to try and get himself under control. When he came back, his advice was right to the point and more than a little graphic. She decided she liked that approach and told him so.

"You're very welcome. And next time we see each other, you should offer me your blood. That way I can speak to you without the use of a phone." She declined. "Suit yourself. But I've been known to be very helpful."

After thanking him again she hung up. CJ was still sitting just where she had been when she gave her the number. Chris liked this woman and told her so.

"I like you too." CJ looked at the door, then back at her. "Sometime I'd like to talk to you about Myles. He's been hurt before, and I wanted to let you know so that it might help."

"No thanks. If he wants me to know, he'll tell me. I'm sure there are things about me he should know, too, but I'm not really the 'share and share alike' kind of girl. I've learned the hard way that knowing too much about a person is simply that, too much." She went through the door and took the stairs two at a time. Time to do it or die. She thought a better choice of words might have been suited but entered the room where he was.

He was lying on the bed with his arm over his eyes. She noticed that he'd closed the curtains too. Going over to the bed she started taking off her clothes. She watched his breathing and knew he was awake.

"I really just need for you to let me rest. Once I get that I'll be as good as new." She stood naked over the bed and reached down and ran her finger over his cock. "Christ, don't do that please. You have to leave Christina, now, please?"

"No." Dropping down to her knees she rubbed her cheek over his hardening cock. "I can't forget how many times I came last night. Christ, you made me feel like a real woman."

"You are one." She heard the strain in his voice and almost grinned when he grabbed her hand. "You're playing around with things that are better left alone. Stop this now."

While he held her hand, she stood and moved over his body, her legs on either side of his hips. When he didn't move, she reached down and tore his shirt open one handed and touched his abs. He was as hard here as he was between her legs.

"You never let me see you last night. I didn't get to touch much of you, but your ass. And, of course, your cock." Running her free hand up from his navel to his nipple she heard him breathing hard. "You're as sensitive as me here aren't you?"

Leaning forward she took his nipple into her mouth. He was breathing very hard now and, when she suckled on it, he let go of her hand and wrapped his hands around her hips. Moving up his jawline she nipped at the pulse pounding there. Myles moaned her name.

"When you bit me, I saw stars. And when you sucked on my throat, I could feel my pussy gushing more cream." She bit again and then moved to sit up. She rode him, sliding her hips over his over and over. The grip on her hips tightened and she rolled her head back and cupped her breast, riding him now with pure pleasure and wild abandon.

"Myles, I need you. I need you so badly." When his mouth closed over her nipple, she curled her fingers in his hair. "I want to taste your cock. I want to feel you come down my throat. Please, Myles. I need you."

His mouth slid along her breast to her throat. She tilted her head back, and he paused just a moment before moving down to her other breast. Reaching between her legs, she worked at freeing his cock, and when she had the zipper half undone, she reached into his fly and wrapped her hand around him. He was thick and wet, his cum spilling from the tip. He begged her to suck him.

She was suddenly on her back, and he was devouring her mouth. Without missing a beat she slid her hand down his pants more until she found his balls. They were tight and hot.

Tearing her mouth from his, she begged him to let her suck him.

Rolling him to his back, she moved down and finished tearing his pants open. His cock sprang free, and she licked the thick stream at the tip. Taking him into her mouth, she suckled at his head and teased the small hole with her tongue. Nothing had ever tasted so good.

He began pumping his hips up, fucking her mouth as she swallowed. His cock slid past her throat and down. Everytime he touched the back of her throat she moaned around him, bringing him to frenzy. Suddenly she was on her back again and he was over her. He opened her legs wider, held her there as he glared down at her.

"Christ, why couldn't you just go away?" He slammed into her. Deep, hard, and filling her to capacity. When she reached for him, he took her hands and put them to the headboard and told her to stay. Then he cupped her breast and bit her. She cried out his name and begged him for more.

"I want to drink from you." He nipped at her breast again and this time drew blood. "I want to nurse from you here and feed. Do you want me to?"

"Yes. Please. I want to feel you bite me again. I want to come when you sink your teeth into me. Take me, Myles." She met each of his strokes with one of her own as he feed from her breast. Nothing had ever felt this wonderful. Nothing ever would, she knew. The harder he fucked her the harder she came back at him. When he lifted his head from her breast, his mouth dripping with her blood, she came.

She pulled him by his hair to her throat. "Bite me. Fuck please, bite me."

As soon as his fang tore into her flesh she came screaming his name. She wrapped her legs tightly around him and felt his cum fill her. Hot, it splashed inside of her, heating her from the inside out. When he lifted his head this time, he reached along his chest and tore the skin. Blood poured from the wound, and he told her to drink.

She pressed her mouth to him and drank from him. It didn't fill her fast enough so she sucked at the wound. She felt him do the same to her throat. Even as she grew dizzy from the sensation of what his blood was doing to her, she drank from him. He came again, and as she slipped over the edge into unconsciousness, she told him she needed him.

~~~

Myles woke with a start. He knew he was alone in the room, yet something had alerted him. He waited, hoping that whatever had waked him would sound again. When nothing happened for several minutes, he lay back down.

He'd drank from her. And as good as he was feeling, it had to be a lot, too. He searched for her with his mind and found her in the kitchen with one of the children. He encouraged her to drink something, and her laughter rolled over him.

"If you came down here, we could enjoy a drink together. When you said you were tired, you weren't kidding, were you?" She was happy, which surprised him. *"You're an amazing lover. And I have never come so hard."*

"Aren't you upset with me for what I did to you?" She laughed again and told him no. *"Why not?"*

"Because it was fucking fantastic. I've never realized that sex could be so fucking mind blowing before. And man can you make a girl feel limp." She laughed again. *"Come down here and be with me. If you don't, I'm going to go back to your house. I have to finish packing. I'm leaving in the morning."*

He leapt from the bed and dressed quickly. He was down the stairs in minutes and walked into the kitchen to tell her she wasn't going anywhere. But the sight of her holding the little boy had his heart skip several beats. Christ, she was a vision.

"He's allowing me to call him Patrick. He said that Mrs. Force named him Josh and he didn't like that. He much prefers the name I gave him. He was telling me that he loves ice cream. I was just trying to figure out what kind when you came in." Myles sat down and watched her. "He knows that I like vanilla, and now you tell him what you like in ice cream."

He stared at her, trying to remember life without her. And couldn't. He was finished fighting her and this thing between them. He had to stop pushing her away and had to convince her that she couldn't leave him. He realized that they were waiting on him and he said the first flavor that popped into his head. "Strawberry. I like strawberry."

Tickling Patrick, she asked him what his favorite was. "Trawberry. I like trawberry like him."

Patrick climbed over the table and sat on his lap. They'd been able to heal the scars on the children's minds but not the visible ones. This little boy had lost his eye. The scarring around it indicated that it had been violent and recent. Myles knew just how bad it had been for him. But Patrick seemed not to notice that he was going to need special care. He was, quite simply, a happy little guy.

Myles knew he'd been hurt trying to get away from Gates. When he'd managed to escape his clutches, poor Patrick had been caught almost immediately. Then he'd been tied to a bed post and beaten with a belt. The buckle had come around and hit him in his eye and shattered his eye socket. He'd hung there for several more hours before he'd been cut down and dropped into the cell again. The other children had helped him as best they could, but more of them had been hurt worse. A lot of them had been taken away never to return.

When Nancy, Austin's mom, told Patrick it was time for his bath, he'd gotten down and ran with her. Myles looked at Chris. She was wiping at tears.

"You like him," Myles said. She nodded and stood. "You aren't going anywhere, you know. I haven't been able to find Gates, and you're still in danger."

"I have a job and I have to get back to it." She shrugged as she started drying the dishes. "He'll just have to either find me or not, but until then I have bills to pay."

"Maybe you didn't understand. I can't let you go. You have to remain here where it's safe. I need to take care of him before I'll even consider letting you go." He knew the moment the words left his mouth it was the wrong thing to say. But it was the truth and he wasn't backing down.

"Maybe I didn't make *you* understand. I have my own life, as you have yours. And mine does not include having some asshole prickly masochist fucktard ordering me around like he owns me. And, in the event that my big words might have confused you, fuck off."

He stood up and she drew her gun. Myles could see the woman standing in front of him in the red haze, but he knew that going after her now might get him shot. He wondered just then if the person who told them that a mate couldn't harm them had ever tested that hypothesis, or did they just hope that everyone would blindly follow along. As she motioned for him to sit, she moved to the door. He started to grab for her, but she fired between his legs and hit the chair seat.

"Mother fuck, are you trying to kill me?" She shrugged and he noticed that the smile on her face didn't reach anywhere close to her eyes. "I demand that you listen to me and sit the fuck down."

"Demanding doesn't really work for me. You should try asking, pleading, or anything but demanding." She opened the door. "If you follow me, so help me, I will make you suffer in ways that will make your head spin."

"Problem here?" She didn't look at Austin, but he did. "Myles, what have you done now to piss off your mate?"

"And that's another thing. Where do you get off calling me your anything? The sex was great, and you've no idea how happy I am that you helped me with the whole coming thing. And feeding you yesterday was fucking amazing, but that does not put us atop a wedding cake, nor does it make us in any way, shape, or form mates." She opened the door. "Now, if you don't mind, I've called a cab. And if my hearing is good, which it is, by the way, that's him now. So until next time."

She turned, but before he could go after her, Austin stepped in front of him and held him back. He was ready to snap at the man to let him go when Chris was backing into the room and she was no longer armed.

Holly stepped in the kitchen next. She had a gun pointed at her and she had Chris's gun as well. When she tossed it on the table, she told Chris to sit. Which, no surprise to him, she did not. A battle of the wills of very strong women was about to begin.

"I said to sit." The compulsion in Holly's voice was enough to make him sit, but Chris seemed to simply shake it off. "You are giving me a migraine. And I hate having a headache. Do you have any idea what leaving now would do to him?"

"And this is all about him, isn't it?" Chris looked over at him as she took a chair. "You starve. Then you shrivel up and die. Yeah, read all about you. But you said you get all you need from food. I'm guessing that I was just a fun fuck and a good meal. Not that I mind. It was good for me too. And as I said, you helped me with a problem."

"He needs blood. Not as much as a full vampire would need, but he does need it. And he won't be able to take it from a bag any longer." Holly looked at him. "You didn't tell her."

"It hadn't come up until now. And as I was never going to bond with her, it seemed stupid that I tell her something that didn't matter. And now that I have, all she wants to do is get herself away from me and I've not had the chance to tell her shit. She's going to do what she wants with or without me."

"Fuck you, you slimy bastard. Feel sorry for yourself much?" Chris stood up. "Why is it that I have to keep getting information about you from other people when all you have to do is open a file with my name on it and you suddenly know me so well? I'm not a bunch of gathered information on a sheet of fucking paper. Since the moment you walked into my hotel room, you've done nothing but order me around and take me places that I didn't ask to go to, and you still have the balls to keep shit from me like I'm some sort of idiot."

"Let her go, Holly." Myles looked at Austin when he spoke. "You heard me, let her go."

Chris was out the door in less than a moment. Myles looked at Austin when he sat down. Myles had started to stand up when he was grabbed hard around the arm. He looked over at the man who was one of his best and closest friends.

"Phil told me once that if I wanted to keep CJ in my life that I had to come clean with her. He said that all the fates in the world cannot make you happy and that if I thought that then I was stupider than he'd first thought. He told me that shifting for her and letting her see the real me wouldn't be so bad. It turned out he was right. Showing her helped us both."

"I don't shift and I'm pretty sure she knows I'm a vampire." He jerked free. "If I wanted advice from a wolf, I'd ask for it. She wants to leave, and there's not a damned thing I can do about it. Hopefully by letting her leave now, I can make some sort of arrangements to go to her when I need something from her."

"Have you told her?" Myles stopped moving at Austin's question. "Does she know why you have nightmares at night? She knows you do. She mentioned them to my mom once. But when asked if she wanted to know, she told her that if you wanted her to know, you'd tell her. She said the same thing to CJ just yesterday. So I ask you again. Did you tell her what happened?"

"It has nothing to do with her. This has no bearing on her case at all." Austin laughed and he turned to him. "Have you told your mate everything about you? All the bad details as well as the good?"

"Yes." That startled Myles, and he turned to look at him and Holly. "Holly has told Phil as well. And if I know him as well as I think I do, Phil has told her everything, too. It's hard to have a relationship with someone and not tell them the good and the bad."

He looked out the door. "She's gone. What does it matter now?"

Holly laughed. "Not really. I told the cab driver to leave, that she'd changed her mind and she's being watched as she makes her way off the compound. I think she might be headed in the direction of Alexis's workshop. The pack is helping her with that decision."

"How?" He closed his eyes when he realized how they were helping her. "You're having them chase her across the compound? Isn't that against some pack law?"

"Not if I'm the alpha. Let her meet up with Alexis. The two of them might come to an understanding. Besides, I think Stacy was headed that way too." Austin stood up. "I'm going to find my mate. All this talk of being together has made me want her in the worst kind of way."

Holly threw a towel at him and called him an ass. Myles sat back down and wondered what to do. Holly patted his hand.

"First thing I'd do is drive into town and buy her about three dozen roses, a box of chocolates and a ring. The ring is up to you, the chocolate, and roses aren't." She got up and handed him the phone. "I think that shop on Fifth is open late."

He took the phone. "And if this doesn't work and she moves back to Virginia? Then what do I do? I can't...I don't want to live without her."

"Then I suggest you buck up and talk to her, then decide if you want to move to Virginia with her or not. She has a nice house, I guess." Holly moved toward the door. "Look, you think you're the only one carrying around a bunch of shit you think someone isn't going to like you for? Grow up and grow some nuts. We all have those issues. The way we deal with them makes us have a better relationship with the people we love."

CHAPTER 7

The building came into view about the time that the pack of assholes faded away. Chris had figured out about ten minutes before that she was being herded. She walked up to the door and knocked. There was noise from the inside, but she heard someone say "come in."

"Hey. Glad they didn't eat you," said a woman at a large stove. She came toward her. "I'm Alexis Force; Gordon is my mate. This is Stacy. She's Dallas's mate." The other woman nodded. "That's Lou. She's Connor's mate and due at any moment. Have a seat. We just ordered pizza."

"So this is another attempt to get me to understand how I can't leave and, if I do, all kinds of shit will hit the fan. No thanks. I've got to get going." Stacy laughed.

"No. Most of the things going on with Myles he's brought on himself. He's a good guy. Just, at times, I think he's trying too hard to take on the world and not heal himself."

Alexis began pouring a hot liquid into molds. The scents coming from them were wonderful and made her think of the little shop in her town. She looked up when she made the connection.

"You're Alexis Dark. You have a shop in the town I live in." Chris suddenly remembered the name. *"Dark Treasures.* You're Dark Treasures. I love your soaps."

Chris flushed when she realized she was being silly. The woman probably had people falling at her feet all the time. She looked around the building and wondered what other things she had here when Alexis handed her a basket.

"Take what you want. I really don't mind. Besides, we're practically family now." She moved gracefully to one of the big crates on a shelf. "This is new. I don't think I've sent any to Virginia yet. You tell me how you like it."

It smelled of oranges and cream. She thought of creamsicles she'd eaten as a child. She started to give it back to her when Alexis put three more in her basket. She was loading the thing up like she was going to stock the store for her. And objecting only had her put more in the basket. She followed along, not saying anything.

"You're here looking for your sister, right?" Chris nodded in response to Lou's question, amazed at how much these people shared with one another. "I wish you luck. The man that might have her, Roy Gates? I've heard he's not a nice person."

"Roy Gates? I don't think...who is he?" Alexis turned to her as Stacy did. "Is something wrong?"

"Didn't you get told who is chasing you? The man that they suspect has your sister?" Chris shook her head. "Have a seat. I'll tell you what we know and what I can't answer, I'll have Connor come and tell you. I can't believe them. Okay. Roy Gates is a very old, very sought after vampire. And not in the good way. He has been on the Paranormal Council's red flag list for, I guess, a few decades. But it wasn't until recently that he's gotten himself onto the 'kill the fucker on site' list."

"He is responsible for the Most Wanted list in the first place, I think. People think that he's been around longer than most old vampire families. The full-blooded families have been talking about his ways of running a realm for more years than Phil has been living." Stacy handed her a picture as she continued. "That's the only picture they have of him. This was taken in the late nineteenth century."

Chris looked at the man, knowing she'd never seen him before. He was sort of good looking, she supposed. But there was an arrogance about him that she could see in his eyes. She handed it back, telling them what she thought, only to be handed another one. This man she'd seen before. And she told her that.

"He came into the station once right before I'd left to come here. He was talking to my sergeant about some dent that was put into his car. I don't know whatever became of it because I was going off shift when my sarge was coming on." She handed her back the picture. "Who is he?"

"His name is Leon Bird. He used to be something of a runner for the man in the first picture. But now we have reason to believe that he is his servant. His original servant had been used to try and keep Myles in France before you showed up." Alexis told her about the man's body and that Myles had gotten away without being questioned.

"And my sister? What do you think she is in all this?" Alexis shrugged. "She is probably making a deal with this Gates person to give me to him for some untold amount of money. She's good at that kind of shit. If it didn't directly benefit her, then she had little to nothing to do with it."

The pizza arrived and the four of them were joined by Dallas, Connor, and Gordon. When the meal was over the men filled her in on more. She sat there for several minutes trying to connect the people. Then she stood up and asked for a sheet of paper.

"I do better with a flow chart." She started writing down the names and the timeframes. Her sister and Gates were at the top, and then she let it flow all the way to the children. She wasn't sure they had anything to do with this but knew that they didn't just show up without a reason.

"Myles said that they had been injured…raped by this Gates person." Chris nodded at Dallas's statement, knowing it was an understatement. "You think he brought them here to throw us off?"

"No. That would only make me want to find out more. And he had to know that we'd get something from the kids even if we didn't have a name or an address. What I think is that someone was supposed to dispose of them for some reason. And, instead of doing that, they brought them here. Why here, I don't know, because as far as I know they don't know that I'm here. And again, this person had to know that we would get something from them if it was the same information I just mentioned. They weren't a ploy. They were something that needed taken care of. Probably nothing more."

"You're more than likely right. It makes the most sense. But Myles does come here, and he's a part of your chart." She looked up at Gordon. "You think that your sister is the key to this. Why? Do you think she'd sell you out?"

"In a heartbeat. The only reason I came here to find her was because she is all the family I have and I made a promise to her mother that I'd keep her out of trouble. Some days I wish I'd never made that promise to her. There are days when I just want to tell her that she's on her own."

When she left the building Gordon gave her a ride back to Myles's house. There were lights on and she dreaded going inside. She looked over at Gordon when he cleared his throat.

"He's a good guy really. A little overwhelmed, I think. When he was killed at that..."

"Killed? But he's a vampire? I didn't know they could be walking around and be killed too."

"That's why he was changed. Phil and Holly changed him when he was killed saving one of the family. None of us wanted to lose his friendship, so we all agreed to let them save him." He looked up at the house when she did. "He also had something happen to him. Something that you should ask him about."

Myles came out onto the porch and leaned against the post. She didn't want to fight with him again and nearly didn't get out. When he stood up and put his hands in his pockets she got out and thanked Gordon for the ride. He drove off before she spoke.

"I'm not going to fight with you anymore. Either we end this like adults, or I walk to town right now."

"I killed a woman the first time I tried to feed. I was starving and she teased me into wanting her. As soon as I bit her I couldn't stop." She didn't move as he took a step down and sat on the steps leading up to the large deck. "I had bitten too deeply and torn her throat. Not only that, but I couldn't seem to stop...sex and drinking blood are nearly the same for younger vampires. I'd not had either since I'd been converted, so I took too much of both."

"You raped her." He shook his head. "Then how did you take too much sex? And why wasn't someone watching you when you fed the first time? I would think that would be standard operating procedure. It's not?"

He nodded before continuing. "I thought I had it under control. I didn't rape her because I didn't get the chance. I did strip her clothes off her and bruise her, but I was never inside of her." He looked to the woods. "She was a hooker, and I thought it would be all right. Not killing her but having sex with her. I'd never...I had never paid for sex before, but I couldn't go to someone I knew."

"That makes sense, I suppose. You wouldn't want the golf buddies telling their girlfriends that Myles Kramer had a dental problem." She waited for him to laugh, but he didn't. "Myles, you didn't set out to kill her. It wasn't your fault."

"Then who's was it? Phil's for changing my life? Holly's for helping him? Or was it the bastard that killed me in the first place?" He stood up and walked back and forth. "I was as good as dead, shot twice. The bullet in my shoulder was bad but not life threatening. But the one in my gut had done a lot of damage. Had I been taken to a hospital with just that, I would have had to retire, but I might have lived. But the man who had wanted me dead had wanted me to suffer, so not only did he shoot me, but he scrambled up my insides like a washing machine. They wanted Phil to suffer as well because we were friends. So this big vampire tossed me against the wall several times and busted me up good. Then he dropped me on the floor to let me die. You have no idea how many times a day that I had wished they'd left me to bleed out."

"Yes I do." He turned to her. "Yes I do. Every day I wish the same thing, that they'd left me in that building to die. But someone had found me after I'd been shot, and they held my hand until the medics arrived. Nineteen people died in that warehouse, but not me. When the prick had been chased into the building I was told to clear, he opened fire to kill me and the others and I froze. I couldn't get off a single shot until those around me were falling. Finally, after he fired over seventy-five rounds, I got one off and into his head. But that didn't change the fact that because of my inability to do my job, I killed nineteen people. But they awarded me with top honors instead."

She turned and walked into his house. She was going to go back home and resume her life. If this Gates person found her, so be it. She was too pissed to fuck with him now. She stopped dead in the doorway when she saw what Myles had done.

~~~

"I wanted to show you that I care for you, something that I've not done very well since I met you." She looked at him, then at the rose petals that he'd put on the floor for her. "Follow them. Please."

She walked along them, and with each of her steps on them, their scent perfumed the air. He could tell she thought they'd go up the stairs, and he'd been tempted to do just that, but this was more important. More important for them both. The door was ajar, and he pushed it open in front of her.

"Holly suggested the roses and the chocolates." He pointed to the large glass bowl on the coffee table that was filled to overflowing with candy bars. "I wasn't sure what kind you liked, and a box of them didn't seem right for you."

"You're right. I'd rather have a candy bar." She reached into the bowl and took one out. He took it from her and handed her another.

"I also wanted to give you this." He pointed to the three large boards that he'd turned around to face the wall when he'd heard the car pull into the drive. "I wanted to have you help me. Us. I wanted you to help us. The sooner we capture this guy the sooner you and I can get on with our lives."

"Do you want to?" He looked at her. "You and I don't seem to get along well other than the sex. And you don't really trust me. I found out tonight that you know a great deal about what is going down, and you've never shared any of it."

He nodded. He hadn't. "It wasn't that I didn't trust you. It's just that I didn't want you to think I couldn't care for you.

You know, be the big macho man. I don't know how to be anything less."

"I don't need a big macho man. I need someone that talks to me. Someone that involves me in what he's doing. You didn't. I found out tonight that you know the name of the person who has my sister."

"Probably has her." He went to the boards and turned them around to face them. "I've laid everything out. The times that we had and some of the pictures we've been able to unearth. Also, over there are some files that I've put together on each person we know is a player."

She walked to them and started to open the candy bar. When she laid it down to pick up a file, he wanted to howl in frustration. As she leafed through it, he took out a bar himself. If she didn't open it soon, he was going to.

"This isn't complete." She handed him a sheet of paper from her pocket. "We figured out this much on Bird at Alexis's house. Oh, by the way, she's gunning for you. She was under the assumption that I was as up to date as you."

He took the sheet of paper and smiled. Christ, she was as anal as he was about timelines. He added the dozen or so times that he'd missed and found an empty file. Putting it in there he went to find information about some of the precinct stuff she had.

"Do you have access to your data base? I wanted to see if there was a report filed on the hit and run with Bird." She told him how to get into it. "There was. It says here that he was hit in the parking lot on West Tenth. That's pretty close to your job, right?"

"Next street. What was the number?" He told her. "That's at the corner. He was close enough to walk to us."

"So what's around there? Any specialty shops? Restaurants?" She shook her head. "What do you think now that he was doing there?"

"Spying? Could be. About that time is when Millie came up murdered. Or so it had seemed. He might have been looking for me. I hadn't seen Millie since my dad passed away about ten years before and only briefly at her mom's before that. Millie and I didn't get along under the same roof and it didn't change after she left home. Her mom had died about a year before my dad. They'd been married about four or five years." He started pulling up other incidents in the area with cold cases. "Hum, Myles, what is this?"

He looked up. She'd opened the candy bar finally. He leaned back in his chair and looked at her. She stood very still, holding the candy bar in one hand and the ring in the other.

"You're a good detective. What does it look like?" She glanced at it and then back at him. "Christina?"

"It looks like an engagement ring." He nodded. "And it looks like you tampered with my bar. It's always been a favorite of mine, too."

"Yes. I did. I wanted to surprise you with it." He got up and walked to her. When he was close, he took the chocolate from her limp fingers and took a big bite, then offered her one. She took it. While she was chewing, he took the ring and bent on one knee.

"I've never done this before. Never actually wanted to until I met you." He took her hand and slipped the ring on her finger. "Christina Collier, will you do me the honor of making me into an honest man? Will you love me as much as I love you forever? Will you keep me on my toes and out of trouble? Will you please marry me?"

She looked down at him and he could see the tears. "Some of those might be hard to do. Like the keeping you out of trouble one, but I'll give it my best shot."

"Is that a yes?" She nodded. "Good. I love you very much."

The kiss was short. She jerked from him so quickly that he reached for his gun. She looked so excited that he smiled.

"I got it. Oh my God, I got it. The children. There seemed to be something that one of you said. He told them not to tell or he'd come back to get them, remember?" He nodded. "He knows where they are. He didn't just drop them off in the woods and hope that they were found. He knew where he was sending them. He didn't hurt them. He sent them someplace where he knew they'd be cared for. He sent them to the big bad alpha."

"You think he's watching them? You think he has someone inside watching over them?" She shook her head as he went to the computer and then stopped. "Do you think he is watching you?"

She nodded. "He knows where I am, I bet. But if he knows, why hasn't Gates come here? He, that Bird guy, for some reason he's not told him. Why not, do you think?"

Why indeed. He got up and looked at the boards. They weren't missing something so much as the dots they had weren't complete. Not for lack of information but because of something they hadn't seen. He was still staring at it when someone knocked on the door.

He looked at her and she shrugged. He motioned for her to back him up by standing on the opposite side of the door while he opened it. He looked in the small hole and saw no one. He jerked the door open and nearly shot Gordon.

"Mother fuck, is that the way to answer the door. You scared the living shit out of me." He handed Chris her bag.

"You left this in the car. And since all your lights were on I thought I'd bring it by. What the hell were you doing that had you so hyped up?"

"Come in and see." Chris moved to stand in front of the door too. She smiled as she put her own weapon away. Gordon looked more afraid of her than he was him. That made him smile.

"You people need a better security system. Or a fucking patrol of wolves running around. They'd tell you not to shoot the first guest you've had here in months. That way people who come by aren't subject to...what the hell happened here? Did you throw flowers at each other as some sort of sexual game?" Myles winked at Chris as they led him into the study. "Christ, you've been busy."

"And we need help." While Chris caught him up on what they'd just figured out, Myles went to see if there was something in the freezer to cook. His phone rang while he was looking. It was Austin.

"I just heard from Gordon. He said you were up and working on this thing with Chris and him. I didn't want to come over empty handed. What can we bring?"

Myles told him anything and Austin said steaks. He told him to fire up the grill so that they could eat when they got there. After he hung up, Connor called. He had the same story. He was bringing drinks. After the fifth time his phone rang with people asking what to bring, he felt Phil touch his mind.

"Having a party? I'm supposed to bring something. I haven't the slightest idea what to bring so I'm going to purchase some potato and macaroni salads. You up for that?" Myles laughed and wondered why any of the Force men, or all of them for that matter, even bothered with phones. They had a great system in place naturally.

"Sure. I think maybe some paper plates too. I've only got three real plates here." Phil growled. *"I'm going to go shopping in the morning. Oh, and I asked Christina to marry me. She said yes."*

"Good. Hopefully she has better taste than you. I'll be there shortly." He paused for a second. *"Are you going to change her? You can if you'd like. You need to have my permission to change her, and I'm giving it to you. If you want it. She would make a fantastic vampriress. Not to mention the sex changes and vastly improves when you're both supernaturals. "*

Myles flushed, trying not to think of their sex life getting any better. She nearly killed him now. *"I'll let you know. Right now, we're going to solve this thing so we can have some fun for a change."*

Grinning, he entered the study. This was going to be a lot of fun. And arguing, no doubt. Was he up for it? Hell yeah he was.

CHAPTER 8

Roy walked around the bedroom. The male that he'd had last night had...well he'd ended up killing him, and he hadn't meant to. He'd been enjoying himself and, when the man had said that he wanted to fuck him, Roy had lost his mind for a second and had freed him. He'd gone for Roy so quickly that he barely had time to slice his throat open, and still he'd been covered in blood. Human blood.

"Sir?" He turned to glare at Leon. "Did you need something from me? I have heard that there was—"

"Where the hell have you been? I have been trying to reach you for hours. And I need this mess cleaned up." Leon nodded and opened the door. Several men and women came in with cleaning equipment and a body bag. As someone carried out the body, several of the others started to clean up.

Roy asked him again where he'd been. "I've been taking care of the other issue. I have also been trying to locate more of your donors. It seems that the orphanages where Daniel had gotten them are no longer in business."

"Forget them. I grow tired of their whining and their neediness. I want you to find the sister. I have had it up to my ass in excuses. She needs to be here soon, and the sooner the better for you. I will be kept updated on information you find, as well. This has been delayed enough."

He nodded and left. Leon was proving to be more helpful than he had ever imagined. And he was getting better every day. He tried to remember if he had ever drank from the little man and decided that he had. How else would he be able to control him so well? Moving to his desk, he looked over the pictures laying there.

Picking up the blurred one of the sister, he tried to make out some of her features and could not. Roy had seen images in Millicent's mind, but he also knew they were old and some forgotten. The two of them had not been in contact, according to Millicent, since a death in the family. He had thought that odd for humans, but said nothing. He had come to realize that if he could he would avoid Millicent as much as possible as well.

But she had been the key to him finding his new would-be lover. But now, he just came to realize, the fucking bitch was nothing more than a whining liar and wondered if anything that spewed from her mouth had a grain of truth in it. He wished now that he'd killed her instead of changing her. But she had intrigued him. So much so that he had given in that one night and had done just what she had wanted. And in return, he was to get her sister.

He had not been sure that Millicent would make the change. Her body had rejected his venom quickly and she had needed more of his blood than he had liked giving her. He still had no idea why he had bothered other than the fact that he hated to fail. And her dying would have been a failure to him.

Training her had been fun. She had taken to his bed quickly but had never really liked having sex with him. That, too, had bothered him. He wanted everyone, especially himself, to be sated after a good fucking. She had seemed bored. That was why, when he wanted to hurt someone, he called for her. Hurting her excited him more than anything ever had. And he wanted to hurt her again.

His cock was aching again. He looked down at it and wondered what Christina would think of his size. Opening his pants, he stroked his thick cock and reached for his phone. He had someone brought to him to relive him. As he waited he wondered if he should go to the little town and find her. The letter that he had had Millicent write was perfect, but his Chris never came to get it. The woman walked in the office just as something occurred to him.

All thought left his mind. She was already naked and her body had been washed so recently that her hair hung in a long wet coil down her back. She stood there with her head bowed and didn't move.

"Come here." She moved toward him and stopped in front of him. He leaned in and took her nipple into his mouth while he moved her hand to his cock. She wrapped her hand around him and moaned when he took the other nipple.

Pressing her down to her knees, he pulled her head to his cock. She wrapped her mouth around him immediately and began sucking him off. Wrapping his hand into her hair, he held her there and called for another male. And he wanted him naked. As soon as he came in the room Roy watched him as his cock lengthened.

"I want you to fuck her from behind while she blows me. When you are ready to come, I want you to come on her ass. I want to see how much cum you have. I will want to fuck you later, and I want to make sure you are worth it." The man nodded and moved behind the girl, lifting her ass up so that she was bent at the waist. "That's it. Fuck her hard."

Roy leaned farther back in his chair to enjoy the show. The man was huge, and the girl seemed to be enjoying herself. When she came, screaming around his cock, the man pulled out and shot his cum all over the girl and him. Roy held her head over him as he came with them. Neither of them moved and he wanted to congratulate them on a job well done, but he did not. He was far too superior to them to let them think he was anything but their master.

"In one hour I will call for you both. But you'll be sucked off by her while I fuck you. And then I'm going to fuck you both in the ass until you bleed for me." He looked at the man who seemed to be ready again. "You prepare her ass for me. I want her so wide that I will need nothing to slide into her. But you'd better not come in her. Understand me?"

"Yes, sir. We'll be ready." As they left Roy put his cock back in his pants. He moved back to his desk and started to go over some of the paperwork that Leon had left for him to work on.

When the door opened later, he looked at his watch. It had been five hours. He hadn't gotten everything done, but he had gotten a great deal moved off and into the trash can. He looked at Leon.

"I do not want you to bring me any more paperwork on my subjects. Most of the shit is petty things that I could care less about. Tell them when they have a complaint to write it out on their own, and you simply trash it. I've no time for making sure that they have enough monies to pay their day help, nor do I care what their excuses are about not having the dues owed to me and the reason why they cannot pay me." Leon nodded. "And as for the girl, have you found her yet? Any information that I should have?"

"I have a lead that tells me that she is with a male vampire. He is said to be a former cop, but I have no information on that as yet. It is also rumored that he has a home on the property of a wolf pack, but that too is not verified." He handed him a photograph. "I have a source that tells me this is the girl."

He snatched the picture. Roy tried his best not to show his disappointment. This girl looked like she had been ridden hard, then put away wet, a term that he had liked and used when he could. He tossed it on the desk with the other picture.

"She has changed a great deal, has she not?" Leon nodded. "I would have thought that she would have gotten prettier not...like this."

He picked it up again. Her hair was short, almost manly. Her nose looked like it had been broken once or twice and had not been healed properly. She was not smiling in the picture, but he could see the sores on her lips like she had been chewing on them and had torn the flesh away. Her skin looked pale, dry and like she had been picking at it with her nails. Roy shuddered and tossed the picture to the desk, making sure that it landed facedown this time.

"Would you still like for me to continue searching for her? I know that you are disappointed." Leon picked up the trash can he had filled. "And the couple you have asked to be ready for you? I believe they had done as you have asked, and the man seems to be hurting. The girl as well. Shall I...what would you like for me to do with them?"

He'd forgotten about them. And that was something he did not want to get around. He looked at Leon and thought that nipping it in the bud was the best course of action. And Leon would make sure that his orders were completed as well as word spread around that he was a man who had no qualms about killing whoever displeased him.

"Kill them both. I want you to kill her first in front of him then... No. I want you to feed them both to the wolves. I do not think they have had a bit of fun for a while. Make sure you cut them up enough that the wolves can find them but not enough that they cannot have their fun."

Actually, Roy hoped to appease the beasts. He was terrified of wolves and with good reason. When he was but a child they had come into his home. His mother and father had been sitting at the table discussing the day's events or some other nonsense while he and his older sister had been working quietly before the fire. The first one had crashed through the opening in the doorway and had gone straight for his father's throat.

His mother had tried to fight it off, but two more wolves had come in the same way, crashing onto the table, pottery flying everywhere. His sister, Rosalie, had shouted at him to run when one came toward them. She ran to the sofa and leapt upon it. The wolf had taken her down and had torn her throat out while he had sat there staring.

The scent was everywhere, as was the blood itself. The cabinets that had been cleaned nightly by his mother were painted with it. It was on the floor in large puddles, steaming in the cold from the broken door. Paw prints smeared in the cooling liquid, and the sounds of them tearing into flesh, his family's flesh, had him move slowly to the fireplace.

The first wolf attacked him. His dark teeth sank into his leg and he screamed. When another tore at his arm, tearing it nearly from his body, he heard someone shout. The wolf was still biting at his leg. It ripped away the flesh and then he stood growling over him. Then he saw them.

Men had come. More than he'd seen in his home ever before. They beat at the wolves, starved and with the scent and taste of human blood on them. A wrist was pressed to his mouth, and he drank even as the others had been hurt and ravaged by the beasts. Looking at the face of his mother, her eyes still open and staring at him, he was told to sleep. Falling away Roy had decided then that he would never be in a place where they could get to him again. Leon's voice brought him back to the present, and he stared at him for several seconds before he realized he had had a memory and nothing more.

"Yes, sir." Leon made it to the door before he turned back. "There is one other thing, sir. Someone has picked up the mail at the post office box. I do not believe it was Miss Collier as I do not think she was given a key to it by my predecessor."

As soon as the door shut behind him Roy laughed. He roared with it until he could not breathe from it. Standing up he went to the darkened window and looked out. The mother fucker had been a major fuck up for some time, and now Roy knew how badly. He decided that it was time for Mr. Oscar to come out of the cell he had him in and pay the price for his insolence. It was time for him to face the sun.

~~~

"The children didn't travel far. And with that many of them would have had to be brought in a bus or a large van." Phil nodded and so did Chris. "So if not that, how else did they get here?"

Chris looked at Myles. "How did you get me to the hospital? On the first day. How did you get me there?"

"I can travel through space quickly." He looked at Phil, his understanding of where she was headed evident. "Is it possible he made several trips to bring them to us?"

"Possible but would have been exhausting. Unless he brought a few and put them to sleep as we had." He looked at the map they'd put up. "I don't remember any mode of transportation in their memories. There would have been fresh ones too. There were none in the children I saw. You?"

"None," Myles said slowly as he stood beside Phil at the boards. Chris looked at him curiously, then at the chart that someone had drawn hours ago.

"You can travel how long without some food? And approximately how far?" Phil said one hundred miles before it would exhaust him. "So less for Myles because he's new."

"Right. And you have to remember that he'd have to travel back, too, so you should shorten that to two and a half. What are you working out?" Myles leaned over her while she did the math. "Ah, so your thought is that he is close enough to bring them the way that we travel. Good. So you think this Leon is a vampire."

"He was at the precinct at dusk. The children were found in the very early morning. If he was old enough, he would be able to be a little stronger than a newbie. So what if he's a vampire? One that works for Gates but isn't all that loyal to him?"

Chris walked to the map of the entire state. She put her push pin on the city where they were and drew a circle around the area she had calculated with a string. Then she made another one about an inch out, then one more an inch from that one.

"This is us." She pointed to the red pin. "And this area is for someone to travel in the least amount of time. Two and a half hours. This one is for three hours and so on. Do we know of any...I can't remember...packs of vampires in these areas?"

"Realms. And I don't know. I'm not required to pledge because of my standing with the council. But I can check." Phil went to the phone on Myles's desk. "I'll call my mom again. She can get information out of anyone. And if she doesn't know it, she will know someone that does."

Myles walked up to her and kissed her shoulder. She looked over at him and leaned into him. The kiss was warm and soft yet hungry and demanding. She pulled back and he suckled gently on her lower lip.

"When I gave this to you, I had no idea we'd be up all night working on it with a room full of people. My plan was to show it to you, then make love to you by the fireplace in our bedroom." He kissed her again and stepped back. "I want this to be finished, and if this is what it takes, then I'm all for it. But I want you."

"I want you too." She looked at the board again. "This will get it over with. Sooner. And all of us working on it together will make that happen. I do have a question for you, though. Will I become a vampire now, too?"

"Do you want to?" Before she could answer him, Phil came up to the board. He handed her a slip of paper.

She marked the first area with a green pin as he explained who the master was. "This is a smaller realm. There are only about thirty or less vampires. The man running it is a friend of my mom. She said that he's a good man and a better leader. She doesn't think he'd have it in him to hurt children."

She put in another pin, this one white. "This one is run by a woman. Also a friend of the family, but she's been having her subjects leave for greener pastures. Her mate accidently met the sun a few decades back when his car flipped over and he was caught in the daylight. She's going to meet the sun, as well, after all her people are taken care of. Again posing no threat that she could think of."

She put a blue one in this area. It was out of the last circle she'd put in, but not by much. Still doable. She looked at him when Phil didn't speak. He looked at her as he explained.

"It's not so much a realm as it is a mansion that belongs to a vampire. There are subjects, but only about a dozen. There have been problems with the place over the years, and mom seems to remember a death, too, of a few humans. She said that one of them was a cousin to my dad."

She didn't know if she wanted the answer, but he nodded when she cleared her throat. "You have a name for this vampire, or do we know it already?"

"No. And mom said she'd look into it deeper, but since this happened, she's been digging and has found only that a vampire owns it. She said that as far as she knew it was still closed up."

"But you don't think it is?" Phil shook his head. "Can we go there and find out? Do a drive-by or something?"

"I don't think that would be wise." She looked at Austin as he spoke up. "There are a pack of wild wolves on the property. So wild that the crew that was assigned to clean the area up surrounding the property a few months ago has never come out. Their truck is on the grounds. The GPS sent a signal until the fall. Either someone tore it out, or the battery died. A few of my pack have had dealings with them, but not much. We're bigger and much more intelligent than regular wolves because of the fact that we can be both at the same time."

"How do you know about the wolves?" She looked at Stacy when Austin did. "You know how? I'm assuming that this land it close to the pack property, and that's somewhat of a problem for you all."

Stacy nodded and frowned. "I ran with a few of them before they were turned. And someone did turn them. I let Austin know so that he would keep the others away from the house and grounds. It's more than a little dangerous; it's lethal to even go near there. They've been tainted with something. Bad magic or simply starved until they would do anything for the one person that fed them. And..." She looked around before continuing. "I think they're being fed bodies. Humans. I could smell it on one of them when they came onto pack land."

Chris sat down and stared at the pin. "It's probably him, isn't it? And we're less than three hundred miles from the place. And he more than likely doesn't know it. Or if he does, then he's only just found out. I'm betting he doesn't know. If he had, then I'm guessing that, wild or not, he'd send that pack here so quickly that we'd be lucky to draw our guns before they killed us."

"Or he would have come here." She nodded at Myles. "Then we have to assume that he knows now. I think if I were you I'd bring on a few more men to watch the perimeter. Also, maybe this is all for nothing, but I would put us all in one place, with the exception of Chris and I."

"And why the hell would we leave you outside of the family?" Austin stood up as he asked. "You think to handle him on your own? Or are you just stupid enough to use yourselves as bait?"

"It's the only way. If he comes gunning for us, we can lay a trap for him here. If he comes to the pack house—"

"You either come to the pack house with us, or we simply stay here in your house until this is over. My house is big enough to stand that many people at once. This one?" Austin looked around. "You don't even have a decent couch, much less a desk. You have noticed that you're using an old wire wheel, right? You come, or we stay. Decide."

Chris laughed. Austin turned to her with a lifted brow. She walked toward him, and he backed up. Smart man. When she was within a foot of him, she stopped and he relaxed. Before he could move, she had him on the floor, his arm behind his back and a gun to his head.

"Can you do that?" He laughed, and she felt the vibration. Suddenly, she was straddled by a large black wolf, and he didn't look the least bit like the man she'd had down. She rolled to the floor, laughing. This man was someone she thought she could trust. All the Force family, really.

"I don't think you can do that either." She looked over at Dallas. "You and he are going to butt heads less if you work together."

She nodded. She looked at him as he moved and then walked with him around the floor. She looked at Dallas again when he cleared his throat.

"He wants to know what the fuck you're doing. He asks me if you're looking for a place to ram a knife." She shook her head. "Then he wants you to back off."

"I can't do that." She looked Dallas. "I don't mean shift, I mean walk like that. He makes no sound whatsoever. He can move without making a sound, and yet, he is huge. See, that's what we both need. You can brute force your way into something. I can shoot my way out. But if we work together, we can be...well, a force of nature."

Austin sat down and stared at her. She got down on her knees and looked at him. She could see him there, Austin the man, and was amazed by it. But the wolf shimmered there as well, and she was pretty sure he liked her. When she ruffled his fur, he growled low, and she laughed.

"You want my help, and I need yours. Together we can do this. Apart we're just a bunch of idiots trying to take down a man that is bigger than any one of us. But we're not just a single person. We're a team. Something that he doesn't have. Look at where he's at." She walked to the board. "No towns, no neighbors around for miles. Wolves that surround the place that I believe you can control if you wanted to. He's secluded and, for the most part, alone. He is there because he is hiding, and what he doesn't understand is that he's given us all the play we need by doing that. A bomb could go off there and few would hear it and probably less would care. It's an empty building as far as they know."

He nodded and looked at Dallas. "He wants to know if you have a plan or are you all puff. His words, not mine. And if you want my opinion, I think you're right. We have to make this work or he'll start coming here and taking what's ours."

Chris nodded. "He's not going to get to that point. As I've heard numerous times in the movies, we're going to take the fight to him."

CHAPTER 9

Myles took Chris up to bed just after sunrise. They were going to meet at two at the compound to go over some of the moves she wanted everyone to learn and teach each other. She and Austin had worked on a list until just before she'd laid her head down to think and had fallen asleep. The others had left right after Austin had.

Laying her on the air mattress, he went to find another blanket. He'd sleep on it until they could get a real bed delivered. When he came back with the only other thing he could find—a towel—she was awake. She smiled at his form of bedding.

"What on earth are you going to do with that?" She stretched, and he felt his tongue thicken in his mouth and couldn't answer her. "Come here, Myles. You're all the blanket I need."

He took off his pants but left on his shirt. He was cold and the room hadn't heated up yet from the space heater. She rolled over him so that she was spread over him and laid her head on his chest.

"We need to get you a bed. This place is bare." He smacked her ass and said it was their bed. "Okay *we* need a bed. *Our* place is bare. And some things for the kitchen as well, like a pan to use. I like to cook."

"We can go tomorrow. Or the next day, but a mattress is something that we need to pick out together since we'll both be sleeping on it." He watched the heater kick on and off a few times. She moved over him and got more comfortable. She'd only managed to make him stiffer.

"I have a house full of furniture. Some of it was my father's that he left to me. Actually, this house was left to me by him. It's a huge fucking house. I can have it shipped here, and that would save us a shit ton of money if you wanted to use any of it. If you don't like it, we can stuff it in one of the other rooms or sell it off. I don't really care." He looked up at her. "I called my boss, Ed Weaver, today and told him that I'd met someone and wasn't coming back. He told me it was about time and to tell you that he felt sorry for you. He's a real prick."

Myles laughed. "So, what are you going to do, Mrs. Kramer, with the rest of your days? You don't strike me as the sitting around the house and eating bon-bons sort of person. But I just happen to know of this firm that specializes in paranormal work that could use another person on their staff."

He'd already talked to the others. Holly was happy not to be the only female on staff, and the others were thrilled as well. He let her go when she sat up on the side of the mattress.

"That would be great, but I don't do charity. You have a job for me, great, but I don't want to…I have some money that can tide us over. Not a great deal, but enough to keep me out of trouble. Well, a little out of trouble. I've never touched the money that my dad left me, and when Alice, Millie's mother, died, she left everything to me, as well. She didn't trust that

Millie wouldn't blow it all, especially up her nose, and have nothing when her husband finally figured out what a waste she was."

He kissed her arm. "I have money, too. A few years ago I helped Austin with a problem he was having with another pack. The guy was a real piece of work. It netted the pack a great deal of money. He split up one quarter of it for his family and that was to be split between them. I was a part of that. He wouldn't take no for an answer." She smiled.

"I can see him doing that. He's a good man. I don't know a great deal about packs and wolves, but I'm betting he's the exception to the alphas. He's a great father, too. His kids are amazing, and he took those little ones in without a question to what it was going to cost the pack to do so."

He rolled to his back and asked her a question that had been nagging at him. "You do know a great deal about our kind. Even before you came here to actually get to know us, I mean. The day in the hotel, for instance. You had silver in your gun, and you had silver handcuffs. How did you know?"

She reached for her bag and pulled out a book and handed it to him. "I love to read, and I started reading a great deal about vampires when I heard from my sister. That author seemed to have a no nonsense attitude about them. And her books are great."

Myles stared at the worn cover and laughed. He was still laughing when he got up and went to one of the boxes on his floor. He dragged it over to her and sat down beside her. He pulled one out and showed her the cover to the one he had.

"The one you have is the fourth book in her series," Myles said. "This is the first one and the rest of them if you want to read them. And here is the series she's written on werewolves. She was dating one when she wrote these. So they're probably as accurate as her vampires are."

She looked in the box and pulled out the second book. She opened it and read the inscription. "You know her?" she asked. Myles nodded. "Are you saying she dated a vampire and that's how she knows so much about them?"

"No, she is one. A very nice one at that. I stayed with her for a while just after I left here a few months back. She taught me a great deal about being a vampire in this day and age and taught me how to save for a rainy day." He looked away. "She is the only person I really ever trusted before you."

She set the books down and looked at him. He didn't know what she was thinking and waited for her to say something. When she did, he laughed again. She was too smart for her own good.

"Just so you know," she said, "if any stories come out that mention an ex-cop turned vampire and he sleeps with the heroine I'm going to stake you. And her."

"I didn't sleep with her. Ever. She thought I was like her son, even though she looks only to be in her early- to mid-twenties. She is one of the most amazing female vampires I know. Now that I think on it, I suppose at her age she could be some sort of relative. Maybe a great-great-great... She's as old as Phil's parents, and I believe they might be in their thousands."

She lay back against him. "We're going to be all right, don't you think? I mean we have had a rocky start, but we're going to be fine. I mean to say that I know that I can be somewhat of a pain in the ass and have the mouth of a trucker on most days, but I'm not too bad once you get to know me. Right?"

"I think you have a lovely mouth, and yes, you do tend to tell it like it is, but I love that about you. And honestly, I think we're going to be great. I believe that we already are." He kissed her. "For as much as I'd like more than anything to make love to you, I don't think this bed will take it. I think that we should get dressed and go into town and have a big breakfast, get us at the very least a mattress to hold us over, then come back here with it and break it in. What do you think?"

She stood up. "I like it. And I'll call my boss and have him recommend a good realtor. He already said he'd make sure my stuff got to me all right. I think maybe he has a buyer in mind for it, anyway. And my stuff won't take all that much to pack. Sometime we'll have to go and get the stuff out of storage, but I'm going to take him up on the deal of helping me out."

He turned on the water, then went and gathered towels. She was still on the phone when he left, and when he returned she was in the shower. Myles quickly stripped down and got in behind her.

"I wondered if you were coming back." She wrapped herself around him and kissed him. "You taste so good."

Moving his hands down her slick body, he turned her in his arms. She was warm from the water, and he ran his tongue down her spine. He pressed her against the tile and massaged her from smooth shoulders over a few gunshot scars and down to her lovely ass.

"You have the most luscious skin. And you taste delicious to me, as well." She moaned when he nipped at her ass. "I want to take you this way. Take you against this wall and come deep inside of you."

Her low growl was all the answer he needed, but he wanted to make sure she was ready for him. Her scent was enough, but he needed to taste her. He took both her hands and put them on the top of the tile and told her to hang on. Moving down to her ass again, he ran his fingers over her seam.

"So wet. I'm going to enjoy this." Spreading her ass cheeks he licked her tight bud. She was moving back toward him, and he smacked her ass. "Be still or I can't enjoy this."

He turned her around and buried his mouth over her heat. She didn't stop moving, and he had to spank her twice more. Every time he laid his hand over her heated muscle, she flooded his mouth with more of her cream. When he took her clit into his mouth and nipped, he pressed his fingers into her pussy and ass and she came apart. Christ, he was going to come from just eating her.

Standing up, she was still vibrating from her climaxes. He lifted her up and took her mouth. He slid her above his cock, then leaned into the wall behind her and thrust into her. He became wild with need and fucked her hard. Over and over he rammed her against the wall until he felt his fangs drop. He had to taste her, had to bite. When she moved her head, gave him her throat, he bit. Her climax milked his cock so tightly he came. Each draw on her vein brought her to another screaming climax. He felt her teeth graze his skin, and he commanded her to take him. When she bit him, tore into his flesh, he came again, this time seeing stars. Christ, she was going to kill him.

After they stood under the spray for a few minutes he reached up and got the shampoo and washed her hair. She was as limp as he was, but she still managed to scrub his back. He kissed her when she scrubbed at his chest.

"I want it." He looked at her, wondering what she meant. "I want you to change me. I want to spend the rest of my life with you as a vampire like you. I want to feel the need to drink from you like you do me. I want to live forever with you."

Myles kissed her again. He had to talk to Phil. He had to figure out how to... He knew there were risks, but he wanted this too.

"I have permission from Phil. He said I was supposed to ask him for it, but he gave it to me because he knew that eventually we may want to take this step. I have to…" He kissed her again. "I love you."

She giggled. "I love you too. But I'm starving and you promised me breakfast. So get a move on, big boy, or I might have to have you for a meal."

That made his heart flip, and he looked at her. He could see hunger in her eyes and knew that if they didn't leave now, they weren't going to. He begged her to hurry. By eight o'clock they were being seated in the only place open. He held her hand the entire meal.

~~~

Leon pulled out his cell phone. He was supposed to check in over two hours ago but hadn't been able to get out of the house. Now that he could, there was no answer. He was getting nervous, and he wanted out of this before anyone else came up missing. Leon watched the couple run across the compound toward the building. This wasn't working any longer, either. He had to figure out a better way to get them out of the house and not on the menu for the pack. Taking one here, then coming back for the other was wearing him down. He was terrified someone was going to find someone he'd left behind and start to ask questions. Like what had almost happened with the children.

His phone rang and he nearly cried out in relief. He answered it cautiously but made sure that the person on the other end had no idea that he was terrified beyond thinking, that he wanted this to end in the worst sort of way. He was losing it, no doubt about it.

"I thought I told you nine not eleven-thirty. How the hell am I supposed to know you're all right if you don't do what you're told?" Leon looked around before answering him. On the tip of his tongue was an answer that would get him hurt, if not killed. He wanted to ask him why he wasn't there when he needed him to be but again refrained from making the comment. Instead, he took a deep breath and let it out slowly before answering.

"I was busy working at cleaning up yet another body. He killed that man you sent me because he fought back when the master let him. He's now lunch for the masses as I will be if I do not get this over with soon." He'd had his body taken to the wolves. The body, like all those before him, had been devoured by them in seconds, and all that was left was the chain that had still been attached to his ankle and the small bit of material that had been on him somewhere.

"He was scheduled for a death sentence anyway, so it matters little how he died. I can send you three more if you need them. One has AIDS and won't last the year, and the other two are also on death row." Hating the cold and calculated way the man had simply dismissed what had happened, Leon told him he could take all three in case they were needed. "Also, the children? What did you do with them? I hope to Christ you didn't feed them to the fucking dogs. If the press ever found out about that, there won't be a hole you can hide in that'll be deep enough." And Leon had a feeling that if the press got any information about any involvement from the agency he was currently working for that Leon would be thrown under the bus.

He looked toward the pack house and smiled. "No. They're safe. I think they're in the best place for now. I don't think anyone is going to find them. I don't believe it would be very wise to have them simply put on the streets. If someone called the newspaper about it the master would surly find out and know that I have not done as he has wished. They'll be fine where they are."

"Good. Good. Now about this shit with Gates or master or whatever the fuck you call him. When are you going to let me have his ass? There is enough dirt on him now that we can bring him in." Leon looked back from the way he'd come.

"I don't think now is a good time." Never would be a good time for him to be turned over to this man or any other. He had plans for the master, had worked on them for as long as he'd been born to do so. No, giving him over to anyone was not the plan. Death was the only thing he could be sure that the master would be gone for good. No one but him knew that the man that the Department of Supernaturals, a new division that was a part of no other agencies, wanted for several murders was an old and extremely powerful vampire and could kick their collective asses without much of an effort. All they thought the master was a vampire of very little power, but a sadistic nature. If only they knew. And no one knew what he was either.

"When for fuck's sake? Do you have any idea how many people are breathing down my neck to get his ass off the streets? Tell me where you are and I'll come and assess the situation. You might just be too close and can't form an objective answer." Leon smiled, glad now that he only took these calls when he was far away from the mansion. "You hear me?"

"Yes, quite well, as a matter of fact. And I am close to it. Then there is the security that is in place here. I'm not sure how you'd get past the wolves if you were to come here. They're very vicious. Not to mention the only time they get fed is when I have to dump a body to them as I have told you." Leon put his hand into his pocket and touched the poison he had been collecting for the past few months just in the event that he did lose control over them. "No. As soon as I have more, I'll bring it to you."

"You need to get more sooner rather than later if you want my continued support. I need more—"

"I have to go. Someone is coming," Leon said after a quick look at the timer. He closed the phone and took out the battery and put both the phone and the battery into the plastic baggie. He put the bag into the tree and walked over to make sure that the couple made it to the big building. He didn't see them anymore and knew that they had made it. He only hoped that they would receive the same treatment as the children were. Kindness and support.

Leon walked back to the clearing. He loved this place of all the land he'd been on. The wolf, the alpha Force, was from all accounts a good man and he hoped someday to explain why he'd sent the others to him. He was glad that when it came to disposing of the children his first thought was of the man. The other alternative would have driven him to insanity, he was sure of that.

Leon smiled when he thought of them, the children. He'd been so troubled about feeding them alive to the wolves. He had thought of the man, Mr. Force, and had felt better immediately. He walked around the wooded area and thought of nearly getting caught.

Millicent had come upon him when he'd come back for the last three. He knew that he'd be tired by the end and had taken as many as he could carry the first time. Then the second time a few less until he had only the remaining ones, the smallest.

"What are you doing with those brats?" He had thought to just put the last to sleep when she startled him. "I asked you a question and I want an answer."

"I do not answer to you, miss. Nor will I ever, no matter what thoughts you have in your head." He picked up the sleeping child. "You can, however, go and ask the master. I'm sure that he will have an answer for you. Though I'm not sure it will be the one you seek."

She looked down the hall that lead to the main house and then back at him. He could see her fear of the master and didn't blame her. The man was mad with self importance. When she stiffened, he nearly smiled at her.

"You'll forget I asked. You may not know this, but the master has a special place in his heart for me. I will not tell him how you treated me this time. But if you do it again…"

"Yes, miss. I understand what you're saying. If there is nothing else, I am to dispose of this." She nodded and scurried away. He looked down at the child in his arms and saw that he was awake. He closed the little boy's eyes with his free hand.

"You will not remember this, child. I will hurt you if you do. Sleep now and I will take you where you deserve."

The low growl startled Leon out of his wandering thoughts. He looked at the beast that stood before him and knew without a doubt that this was a man, not a wolf. He turned to see if there were others and didn't see any.

"I'm not here to harm any. I am merely passing by." He started to back up when the wolf growled again. "You don't want to harm me, sir. I have been…I am needed or others, like the children I sent to the compound, will die."

The wolf sat on his haunches and looked at him. Leon waited for the wolf to let him go. Leon knew enough about wolves to know that they would kill and kill quickly. But these wolves, werewolves, he did not know as well as the wild ones around the house. The wolf lay down. Leon nodded.

"I have sent a man and a woman to you. To the building far off. You will see to their needs without telling anyone?" The wolf nodded. "Thank you. I am in your debt."

Leon knew that the big black wolf followed him. He didn't blame him. He was a stranger in a strange place. When he was as close as he could be without anyone knowing where he came from he looked back at the wolf.

"The children? They are well?" He nodded again. "Your alpha, he is a good man?" The wolf nodded again and looked away to his left. Leon disappeared in that instant and made his way to the mansion to see to his master. There was much to be done and very little time left in which to do it. He heard his name bellowed through the hall and went to the mad vampire.

CHAPTER 10

"I'm telling you he was a really nice man. Polite and asked about the kids and so on. He said you were a good man too, but right now I'm beginning to have my doubts." Chris looked at Austin, then at Connor. "He said that he sent us a couple. I'm assuming it was those two that ended up at Alexis's. Why would he tell me that if he had an ulterior motive? Especially when he told me who and what they were. They were humans, and they were starved."

"Yes, but that doesn't make him a saint, it just makes him honest. He dropped those people off because he wants something from us. Something…I don't know." Chris snorted and Austin looked at her. "You have something to add to this conversation, or do you need a tissue? I'm beginning to think you have allergies or something the way you keep doing that all the time."

"Blow me, big boy. And I do have something to add if you'll shut up long enough for someone else to get a word in edgewise." He growled and she grinned. "You really are an old softy, aren't you?"

She wanted to pinch his cheeks but was sort of afraid she'd come back without a hand or, at the very least, one or two fingers missing. But she did enjoy his way of getting around things. He was firm and had an open mind, too. Not a combination she'd encountered much in her line of work, a sort of all boys club.

"What do we know about the couple other than they were naked as the day they were born, starved, and human." Something occurred to her when she said that. "By the way, I'm hoping we come up with a term other than 'human.' Can't we just call them adults? Most of us are, with the exception of a few I could name."

She looked pointedly at Austin. His growl made her laugh again, and she watched as CJ covered her mouth with her hand and coughed her way through a spell of laughter of her own. Then, when CJ moved to the fridge to get him a glass of tea with some sugar, she smiled. Chris doubted it would work at sweetening him up but it was worth a shot.

"I'm thinking that we need to have cooler heads." CJ looked at her and winked. "And a tad less poking the bear, Chris."

"Sure, no poking the bear. Got it. That leaves big bad alphas wide open, right?" She leapt from the counter when he came after her. They had been sparring all morning and she felt she was getting the better of him. She moved out of his reach only to come up on a hard body. Without turning she knew it was Myles.

"Behave if you please. You're making him pissy and we still have to live here." Myles kissed her shoulder and nipped none too gently at it. "The man that Connor saw is the same man that brought the children to us. So now we have a name to associate with him."

Myles sat down and she went to him. The need to touch him was overwhelming. She looked around the room and noticed that most of the others were touching their mates and looked at Nancy. Chris rubbed her forehead without thinking. She'd been bobbed in the head with a wooden spoon earlier by this woman and didn't want a repeat performance. And all she'd done was suggest that maybe she and Myles find another place to stay for the duration.

"Some of them have names. The children I mean. The younger ones didn't know at first, and the others said that they had been given numbers from the time they had been at the dark place. None of them, it seems, have any memories of the place they'd been before. But they do remember being a part of an orphanage. From their description, I would say that it was the one that closed last year because of the poor conditions they were keeping the children in." Nancy offered her a sandwich and a glass of juice. "They are remembering more from before but, thankfully, have no recollection of the life they had prior to coming here."

"Are they doing okay now? I heard that one of them, a small boy, is having nightmares nearly every night. Is he doing okay?" Nancy nodded. "Can I talk to him?"

"Of course. He is the little boy that you named Patrick. He said you called him that and he wants to keep it. I believe he is playing in the den with the others." Chris went to find him taking her sandwich with her. He came running to her when she sat down.

"How are you, buddy? Are you having fun with the other rug rats?" He nodded. "I wanted to make sure you were getting everything you need, and I wanted to talk to you about something. Mrs. Force said you were having dreams. Can you remember them?"

He yawned and smiled at her. "A man was holding me. He was talking to someone, and they were going to feed me to the wolves." He looked around. "I don't know what a wolf is, but David over there said they had great big teeth and they eat little kids for breakfast, lunch, and dinner."

He sounded more amused than afraid, and she ruffled his blond hair. She looked up when Patrick looked over her shoulder and saw Myles coming in. She had a moment to wonder how long he'd been there when he sat and spoke to Patrick about wolves.

"They're large canines, sort of like dogs but not. They can be very scary, but sometimes they aren't. Sometime, I'll let Christina show you one and you can pet him. You might even get to run with him." Patrick nodded eagerly and yawned again. "You have any more ice cream?"

"I have to eat all my dinner first. Mrs. Force said it's good for me." He laid his head on her shoulder. "I'm very sleepy. I just need to rest my eyes. I'm too big for a nap."

In a few minutes he was asleep and Chris looked over at Myles. "Can you see who Leon was talking to through him? It might be the vampire we're looking for. He might have seen him."

"I can look, but I wouldn't count on much. He said himself he was afraid. And the threat of wolves, even though he didn't know what they were, might have made him focus on something that wasn't there." She nodded and watched as he put his hand on Patrick's head gently without waking him.

Myles didn't say anything for several minutes but simply watched the little boy. After a few more he looked at her. When he closed his eyes, she knew that he was taking the memory from Patrick as he had the other nightmares the little guy had. He leaned back against the couch after a few more minutes, taking his hand away. He looked nothing like he had after the first time.

"It wasn't the vampire. He saw the person only for a few seconds, but he saw them together. It was Leon who held him along with two other children. And just as we thought, he'd carried them in lots so that it would be easier for him. The two smallest ones and Patrick were more than likely the last of them, as they were the lightest. It's what I would have done." She knew he was trying to brace her for the news, and she suddenly knew who it was.

"It was my sister, wasn't it?" He nodded. "I see. So that means she has been helping him and she has been a part of this from the very beginning."

"She might be his captive too. You don't know." She did and told him so. Her sister was always one to come out on top no matter who she had to stomp on to get there. She looked to the other room where the rest of the Forces still were.

"We have to tell them. They have to know that she's the one feeding him whatever information he needs to get me." She leaned on his chest after sliding Patrick to the couch beside her. "What could he want me for? I don't hold any special powers. I'm not all that special. All I have is the money that our parents left me."

Her money. She was doing this for her money. She looked at Austin when he walked in. He smiled at her, then frowned. The man was entirely too perceptive.

"What happened? Is it one of the children?" Chris shook her head. "Then what? Is it that you're just coming to realize that I'm all that, or is it because I was getting better at this defending stuff and you finally realized that I can take you?"

He was trying to lighten the mood, and she smiled at him. "I can take you with one hand tied behind my back, and you know it. No, dork face, it's something else. But it could be harmful to you and yours. My sister is with the vampire. She was seen by Patrick when he left. I think she's doing this because of the money her mom left me and not her."

"Her mom left it to you? Why did her mom leave you money?" Austin looked at Myles. "Am I missing something here?"

She answered before Myles could. "My sister is a flake. She goes through money like it's her job. When her mother, Alice, died a few years ago, she asked me to watch over Millie and try to keep her out of trouble. She left me the money so that I could bail her out when she needed me to. I guess her mother was right on that one, but I don't think there's enough money in the world to get her ass out of this one. But when my dad died, I sold the house she had already owned when my dad married her and put that money with the rest. I've got a good job, and I didn't even touch the money that my father left me when he passed away, so it just added to the nest egg I was building on."

"Shit. That sucks." She smiled at Austin. "Okay, that makes things easier, I suppose. Now we have a reason and a working knowledge of what he knows. And since you said you've not seen her in years, her information is old and probably half truths, anyway. But as I said, we know where he gets his information. Did you get the feeling that Patrick thought that her and Leon were buddies?"

"No, on the contrary, I got the feeling that Leon thought she was beneath him. She tried threatening him and he told her that she should go and see the master. She didn't seem all that pleased with his answer." Myles sat up. "You think that she's on borrowed time, as well? Gave you up as sort of a way to appease the master? And it's not working?"

Chris could see that too. She was so hard to live with when Chris was a child, always whining and conniving to get her way. Her dad had seen through it right from the beginning and had basically told Millie on several occasions that she was a liar and a thief. A thief of his time in having to try and sort through her lies took time from him, and he didn't appreciate it. Chris thought that was why she had always been a straight shooter. She didn't want to steal time from a person.

Connor and Gordon walked in just then. Gordon looked at her, then at Austin. He smiled. There was something so boy-like despite the fact he was a lethal weapon.

"It could be that he simply wants her. I'm serious. You're young, beautiful, and built. I'm betting your step-sister is probably a little good looking, right." She looked at Gordon and laughed when Alexis glared at him. "Not as well as my mate, but you'll do, I suppose."

"Good save," Alexis said as she sat down beside Chris. "But he might be onto something. What's to say that it's a simple case of lust for both of them? Stranger things have happened. Say he was looking through your sister's memories, and poof, there you are. Someone younger than the bitch he has, prettier, and a sight less used in this case. What does she look like?"

Myles handed her a picture. Then after she looked at that one, he handed her the file which she went through quickly. Chris had helped, too, with a few from her wallet, but none of them were up to date, either. She looked at Alexis when she handed them back to her.

"Okay, yuck. Has she heard of acting her age? What is with that purple streak in her hair? And those clothes?" Alexis shivered. "And then there is the fact that you're not a lying sneaking bitch."

"Thank you, I think." Chris looked at Myles. "Something's been bothering me. Could she or someone like her have manipulated Peter into saying he killed her? Then maybe had him kill himself later? I read about that in one of those books I had taken from the library before coming here and wondered if any of that is true."

"Yes. It's very possible. She could have made him do whatever she wanted in a very short order of time even as a new vampire with someone there to help her. She could even go so far as to have him write out the confession. That way they had a reason for her body to have disappeared." Myles looked to be warming to the idea. "Why didn't you get the mail at the post office?"

"I didn't have a key to it." Myles nodded. "And when I went to the desk to ask about it, they said that I needed the person on the account to give me a copy or to have her be there to tell them that I could have it."

"Of course. But there was a key. Daniel Oscar had one in his possession when he was taken to the morgue. It was a mailbox key but nothing on it to say what box or post office it went to. I read it in the report." He disappeared, and she fell to a chair, then nearly leapt out of it again when he appeared before her. "Here, see?"

"Don't do that again." He looked at her oddly, then around the room. "You can't just go bye-bye like that without saying good-bye or something. But you can't...Christ oh mighty."

"I'm sorry, love. I was so excited that I didn't think you'd ever seen me do it before." He laid the folder down and took her hand. "I didn't think."

She nodded, then reached for the folder. She had been terrified that someone had taken him from her. When she felt the tiny push into her mind, she looked around the room to see if anyone else was feeling it. They were having a good time teasing Myles. Then she heard a voice she never thought to hear in her mind.

"Hello, sister dear." She grabbed a pencil and wrote "Millie" on it and shoved it at Myles. *"You have been a very naughty girl, haven't you?"*

"I don't know what you're talking about." She spoke out loud when Myles looked at her and nodded. "Where are you, Millie? You said you were changed and that I needed to come to you."

Her laughter made her skin crawl. *"I'm with the greatest man I've ever met. He makes me feel things that you can't imagine. He's wonderful and he loves me."*

She looked at the note from Myles. It simply said to "Piss her off?" She thought about that and wrote back "mention vampire?" He nodded.

"You mean Roy," she asked her sister. "I hear that he is a real piece of work. Much like you in that department, I guess, so it's no small wonder that you get along with him so well. But there is something I wanted to ask you. I want you to tell me why he's trying to have me killed. Or do you even know? You always did seem to have a knack for saying things you never knew the truth about and spewing back answers that have nothing to do with anyone but you."

"Why, Christina dear, he doesn't want you dead, he wants to fuck you. He wants to make you like me and him. He wants me to bring you to him so that he can have us both. And I'm going to do just that. We'll be lovers with him. Won't that be wonderful?"

"No, that would be gross. So I happily have to decline both your offers. Besides, I've had vampire, and I'm pretty sure that Roy boy is gonna have to find someone else to be his bread in this sandwich. I'm not coming." She looked at Myles. "You tell him to girth it up, because as of right now, I'm coming for both your asses. And when I do, I'm bringing silver and a shit ton of kick ass too."

"You'll come here because I told you to. And I'm your sister and mom told you to take care of me. You'll also bring me what's mine. I want that money, and I want all of it or so help me I'll...I'll..."

"At a loss there, Millicent? You never could think on your own. That's why your mother didn't trust you, and neither do I. You think you can get me? Bring it on bitch. I'm ready for you." Myles touched her head and the connection was broken.

Chris felt weak, and her head was pounding. When a glass of juice was shoved in her hand, she drank it and the second one too. She looked up at Mrs. Force when she handed her a third. The spoon in her hand made her take the glass rather than tell her no more. Chris was afraid of that thing more than she was a room full of drug addicts and they just figured out she had an ounce of heroin on her and were set to get it from her.

"I think I pissed her off." Mrs. Force laughed. "I can't drink any more. But I could use something for my head."

"It's because you were speaking out loud. If you had spoken to her the same way, you would have had a slight weakness but nothing more." Myles held her hand while a bottle of pain reliever was opened for her. "Are you all right?"

"Yes. Why did I just piss off the mistress to a vampire? Am I really that stupid?" Everyone laughed. "I know you're going to say because pissy people make mistakes, but my head hurts too much for me to think what it was."

"She said that he doesn't want you dead, but to have you in his bed. That has to piss off your sister when she just told you that he was in love with her." Chris nodded. "And she wants her money."

Mrs. Force handed her another glass, this one water. She smiled at her as she spoke in low tones. "It seems you've been a very busy girl since you came to our little town. You've not only taken all her money, according to her, but her man as well. Not much left for it, but you have to go show that woman that you've done a sight better and that you don't need her money."

Chris took the pills and stood up. Mrs. Force was a lovely woman, and she was as straight a shooter as she'd ever seen. She hugged her and was happy when she hugged her back.

"I could really get to love you." She smiled at the elder Force.

"I could certainly love you as well. And I most certainly do. Even though you are somewhat of a stubborn woman and a pain. But you love Myles, and that counts for a great deal." Mrs. Force kissed her on the forehead.

"You know that I'm going to find that spoon and burn it, right?"

"You and a bunch of others have been threatening me with that since my mother gave it to me on her deathbed. But only I know where it is, and nobody's going to take it." She touched it to her forehead with a small brush of her lips. "You wait and see you don't have one for your own kids someday."

~~~

Millie screamed around the room for over an hour before she felt she could go and talk to Roy. Her cell looked as if a large tornado had blasted through, and Millie didn't care one bit. She would simply get more of what she needed. No one knew all the things in this house anyway, and when she found something she liked, she simply took it. Roy, she was sure, would want her to have it. But he was going to be mad about the conversation she'd had with Chris.

He'd told her not to mess this up, for her to make her sister come to him now, willingly. Millie would have to explain to him again what kind of person her sister was and hope that he understood. Her sister was stingy, mean, and had a streak of vindictiveness that Millie hated. And what was worse was that Millie could never make her sister believe anything she told her even when it was the truth, which wasn't often. She went to Roy's chamber and was bid enter when she knocked.

"You contacted her?" The eagerness in his voice made her mad. "Have you convinced her to come here to see you?"

"She is being stubborn. I told you what she is like. She said she'd come if I paid her for it. I've never met a greedier woman in all my life. The nerve of her wanting me to pay her for a visit. I'm her sister, and she should want to come to see me." Millie was going to get something out of this deal even if she had to go and steal her sister away to get her here. And money was going to help her when she got out of this ugly place.

"How much does she want? Whatever it is, she can have it. Double whatever she asks for if that's what it takes. I don't care. She can have it. I want you to contact her and tell her that whatever sum she wants, it's hers." Millie nearly told him she'd take it to her, but he continued. "She won't have any use for it once she comes here anyway. Once I make her mine, she'll want for nothing."

"You plan to make her your mistress?" He shook his head, and she felt relief. He wouldn't do that to her. Not after all she'd done for him. She sat down on his bed thinking to thank him for that bit of information by letting him take her as he had the other day. It had hurt more than she ever thought possible. But she had healed quickly, and now that she knew that, he could do it again.

"I plan to make her my bride," he told her with a soft sigh. "She won't have my children, of course, as she isn't my true mate, but we can make them for us. Take some that humans would only ruin and make them ours forever. She and I together will be as one being, and I will give her all that I am. I will even pay for her to have some surgery to make her more beautiful so that when we go into public together, she will be so proud to be by my side." He looked at something on his desk and handed it to her.

She looked at the picture he'd handed her and frowned at it, then at him. "This can't be Chris. She's too...well, Chris is a hard ass, but she would never let herself go like this. And her nose is all wrong. Not to mention, this woman looks like a hooker somewhere. Chris was lovely even as a brat kid. This woman isn't her. I don't know where you got this, but this isn't her."

At first she thought him angry with her and cringed when he snatched the picture from her. When he called for Leon, she thought he was going to tell him to feed her to the wolves. She looked at the window that had just been replaced and turned to Leon when he walked in the door.

"Yes, sir. I was just coming to see you. I have another bit of information that you asked me to collect." He handed him a file. "It only just arrived on the fax machine just now. I think you will be pleased with what has come in."

Roy sat at his desk and looked over the information. Millie inched her way to the door. When Roy said her name, she tensed and turned back to him. His smile made her feel like she had been caught at something. And as there was plenty that she could be caught at she was terrified beyond fear. She was quaking in it.

"It seems you were right, after all. That wasn't your sister. Leon has been doing an excellent job keeping me informed and he just found this." He handed her another picture. "Is that the sister you remember? She's quite lovely. In fact, I would say she's the most beautiful woman I've ever seen."

She handed it back with shaking fingers and said it was her. She looked at Leon, and he winked at her. He knew. She had no idea how he knew that she was about to get him into trouble, but he did. Then he just happened to have those pictures on standby to bring in to turn the tables on him. The man was making her life difficult and she didn't understand why. Everyone usually gave her what she wanted except him and her sister. She stomped her foot, and Leon looked at her with an amused smile.

As she walked back to her cell after being dismissed she vowed to get Leon. And Chris. Those two were not going to treat her like this and get away with it. Neither was Roy. It wasn't her fault that Chris had turned out more beautiful than she'd remembered. And Millie knew that Chris was coming here to throw her away like she'd made her mother do all those years ago. Millicent Newman was not going down without a fight or, at least, without her pound of flesh. They were all going to pay.

CHAPTER 11

Myles kept an eye on the delivery men. He hated having all these people in and out of their home, but knew it was necessary to get things set up for his and Chris's home together. The men were setting up the bedroom when she came out of the kitchen. She was smiling and he couldn't help but smile back.

"He did a great job, didn't he? Ed has been getting my mail for me and said that he talked to a realtor the first time I called. He said that getting someone to pack up my shit was a breeze. He's already got a buyer for the house." He watched the next load of stuff come in as she continued. "You're okay with this, right? I mean I know it's a lot for you to handle. Going from your lovely yet sagging lounge chair to real furniture can be quite a shock to the system. Especially to your poor ass."

"Very funny. And I'll have you know that I picked that sucker up cheap because it was on sale, not because it was sagging. That came later. I just had no idea that you had this much." He looked at the once bare living room and loved the change but had to give her a hard time too. "I mean who can

131

stand all these neutral colors? Why not some bold blues and greens? I was actually thinking of painting this room puce."

For a couple of seconds, she believed him. He could see it in her face. He pulled her into his arms and held her as another load of stuff was brought in. He walked to the dining room with her to have some privacy. She'd unpacked it first and Myles was again blown away by the difference that some furniture could make.

The table was old and oak. He ran his hand over the smooth surface and marveled at something so lovely. There were six chairs down each side and one at each end. There were two others against the wall that matched the table. He looked in at the pretty dishes that were all set up and glowing under the light and knew that they had special meaning to her.

"They were my grandmother's. I was given them when I moved out on my own. They've been in storage since. I had no idea he had cleaned that out until this box was brought in. There is more in the kitchen."

The kitchen had a refrigerator and a microwave...a broken microwave on the counter when he lived here alone. He looked around the room and couldn't believe it was the same room. There was a tea maker on the counter and a state of the art refrigerator in the place of his smaller, much older one. She told him that she'd had his taken to the garage when she'd seen how big hers was. There were pots and pans hanging from the rack that he'd been hanging whatever struck his fancy on before. Cook books lined the shelf beneath the butcher block that had been overflowing with pizza boxes just yesterday. He looked at her when she touched his arm.

"You can take out whatever you want. It's just stuff. I swear I won't mind." He laughed when he looked around again. "I'll even have them bring your refrigerator back in."

"I really love it. I've never seen a house come so alive. I want you to be happy and this stuff," he said as he swiped his hand around the room, "this makes me happy too."

The movers were hanging the television when he went back into the living room with her. Christ, it was huge. Walking over to see how the men were doing, he spread his arms wide and still couldn't touch the edges of it.

"This is going to be great to watch the Bears play on Sunday afternoon. A few beer and some snacks. We'll—"

"Green Bay. We'll be watching the Packers." She skirted around the big couch to take the remote from one of the men. "See? I have it fixed so we can watch every one of their games. Green Bay."

"No, no, no. We'll be watching the Bears play. Chicago Bears. You'll love them." She was already shaking her head. "Come on, you can't be serious?"

He wasn't. He didn't care what he watched in the name of football. And he'd seen the throw she had put in the blanket chest that had Green Bay on it and wanted to yank her chain. He just loved a good game. She tossed a pillow at him and one of the workers laughed.

"You can't think that a man would give up his team, would you?" The man looked at Chris, then back at him when Myles had engaged his help in the cause of the Bears. "I mean, it's the Bears."

"I don't know, mister, but I'd be watching whatever she wanted if'n she was to want to snuggle up with me to do it." The man flushed. "I'm not saying I would. I'm just saying that she's really pretty and all and... I think I'll shut up now and finish the job."

Myles laughed and told him he was right. He walked toward Chris and took the remote from her and tossed it on the couch. He kissed her mouth, then pressed her against his body.

"Of course we could watch porn one day and try a few of the moves we see there. Could be educational." He wagged his eyebrows at her. "Nice fire in the fireplace, porn on the television? What do you say?"

"I say you should behave yourself before I have them take the television and the cable away." She kissed him again. "We have a smaller television in our bedroom if you want to watch porn."

He laughed. He realized that he'd not laughed this much even as a human and marveled at the difference a mate could make in such a short time. He looked around the house and also realized this wasn't a house any longer, it was a home, their home.

The eight movers came down the stairs and told them they were finished. They just needed to go around to each room with one of them and inspect it. Both Chris and Myles followed the foreman around and looked into each room. Myles hadn't realized that there was enough furniture in the two moving vans to fill all five bedrooms.

He looked into each one, vowing to come back and look closer at each room. He already fell in love with the blue one. He needed to talk to her soon. Myles thought that this one would be perfect for what he had in mind to use it for.

When they walked to his study, they looked at the large desk and he walked over to it. It was brand new, the blue plastic to protect the drawer covers still in place. The desk chair was wrapped in a white cloth that had the store name on it. He looked at Chris when the movers and the two of them walked out.

He tipped the men, giving each of them a hundred dollars. He knew what it was like to move furniture and he had the money to spare. The men were happy when they left and he was thrilled when they did. He closed the door behind them and looked at his lovely mate.

"You bought me a desk." She nodded. "And a chair. What else is in those boxes in that room that you didn't let them open?"

"I wanted you to have something new." She moved to the study. "Your computer is as old as me and you were using a wire roll for a desk. There might be some other things in there to help you with our business. A few toys that I had when I worked for the department before leaving and a few that I had Ed picked up for me and sent along."

He opened the first box. It was not just a computer, but a very expensive one. A twenty-seven inch monitor and wireless key board and mouse, too. The speakers, he knew, would really crank out the tunes. There was a mid-sized printer as well as a fax machine and two cases of paper, along with a filing cabinet that matched the cherry of the desk and the boxes of file folders that were still in boxes on top. He looked at her as she played with his chair.

"I think this is a perfect opportunity to break in this sucker, don't you?" She stared at him and he saw her eyes darken. "I could bend you over this thing and see if it'll hold all the weight of all the jobs we'll be doing together."

"Yes. We could do that." She ran her fingers over the desk and made his cock twitch. When she sat on it and leaned back, he nearly went to her to beg him to let him fuck her.

Myles watched her move. Like a cat. He wouldn't have been surprised if he touched her that she didn't purr. When she lay down he walked to her and stepped between her open legs. She started to sit up and he told her to lay back.

"I might as well try out my chair while I'm at it, don't you think?" He pulled it up to where he'd just been standing and sat in it. "Christ, this is the perfect height for what I want to do to you."

He pulled her to the edge and set her feet on the arms. Reaching up under her skirt, he touched her panties and found them soaked. He pulled them off her hips and then her legs. Myles put them over his shoulder, already hard as stone to take her. The skirt was next. He flipped it up and over her belly so that she was spread before him like a Thanksgiving dinner. He moved forward and touched his tongue to her thigh.

"I'm going to love this," Myles said as she moaned. "I want you so badly, but this can't wait." He licked a path from her knee to her mound and up the other leg. He didn't touch her yet; he wanted her to beg him. Or he begged her. He thought he might be the first to cave.

The pounding vein in her thigh called to him. He told her what he was going to do and she moaned again. He licked the pulsing vein, sank his fang into her, and drank deeply. He slid his finger into her and tasted her excitement in her blood. After sealing the wound, he went to the other leg and bit her there. Her climax made her tighten around his wet fingers.

He then moved to her nether lips and nibbled on them, tasting them. His fingers continued their movements as he released his cock with his free hand. He wanted to fuck her like this, take her hard, and have her scream out her release with him. But he wanted to drink as much of her into him as he could first.

When she came again, he suckled her clit into his mouth and pushed his tongue into her pussy along with his fingers. Each time she cried out he slowed his movement until she regained control. He, on the other hand, was losing his quickly. He stood, pulling her up with him, and bent her over the desk.

"I want to see you naked like this. Your clothes in shreds on the floor around us." He nipped at her shoulder through her blouse as he continued. "Is anything you have on expensive, something you treasure?"

"No, please. Take them off me, Myles. I want you to take them off me now." He tore them from her. The blouse was in tatters and the skirt didn't fare much better. Her breasts, unfetter by a bra, bounced freely.

Taking his cock in his hand, he moved behind her. "I'm not going to be gentle. I want to take you hard." She nodded.

He grabbed her hip and slammed into her. When he was fully seated, he held her with both hands at her hips and pulled out of her to the tip of his cock and took her to the desk top this time. He was leaning over her when she cried out. He was so close that he knew he had to take her completely. She begged him to take her. And when his cock exploded inside of her, he bit her hard in her throat.

He emptied into her. Never had he felt so completely sated and yet needing so much more from her at the same time. His cock hardened again while still deep. When she licked along his wrist, he knew that if he never in his life thought of nothing else in this room, her being beneath him would be it.

He opened his wrist after sealing the wound in her throat and pressed it to her mouth. He came again, though not nearly as hard when she took his wrist greedily. He held her to him as she finished taking what he'd taken from her before pulling her to his lap and sat down. Myles sealed the ragged wounds himself and rested his chin on her head and closed his eyes. He held her like that until she spoke.

"Phil talked to me this morning. He told me that you are going to change me when this is over." He nodded. "I was wondering if you could tell me what to expect?"

"I don't know. When I was converted, I was dead. Or as close as one could get, I suppose. I didn't hurt, if that helps. Phil said that there could be pain if it's not done correctly. But he said that I would, he'd make sure of it. He said he'd be with us when we did it." He looked down at her. "Are you afraid?"

"No. It's not that. I'm more afraid of the idiot that is coming for me than you making me your vampire bride. Tell me what you're going to do." He opened his mouth to tell her when someone knocked at the door.

"Are you fucking kidding me? Who comes to a house…well, I was going to say late, but it's only four o'clock in the afternoon." He stood up and started to pull at his clothes. "But seriously, who does that?"

Laughing, she wandered around the room, picking up the pieces of her clothing. "Who cares? But I have nothing to wear. And you look like you've been fucked hard. Why don't we wait in here until they leave, then go up and get our clothes and put your office to rights?"

He liked that idea and they waited. When nothing else sounded, they snuck up the stairs from the kitchen and went to their bedroom. After pulling on some old sweats and a t-shirt they went to the office and worked until it was completely set up. And they had a great deal of fun while they were at it. Finally, after gorging on Chinese food that Myles had gone to get with his powers, the both laid back on the floor.

"I'm beat." He looked at his watch. "And it's after midnight. How about we hit the hay and then set up whatever else is left in the house tomorrow?"

She yawned her agreement. They were walking hand-in-hand, then he ran back down the stairs and set the security. He ran up behind Chris, picked her up, and carried her to their bedroom. They were both asleep within ten minutes after the light went out.

~~~

Roy paced. He wanted some answers, and he wanted them yesterday. When he heard a noise outside his chamber he bid whoever was there to come in. He was disappointed to find Millicent there.

"What is it you wish, slave? I have better things to do than to listen to whatever small complaint you have this eve." He heard her sharp intake of breath but didn't turn from the darkened window.

"Complaint, sir? I have done nothing but try and please you. I have given you everything and have worked hard at making this a home for you and my…and my sister. And do you still think of me as a slave? I thought we had moved beyond that to something—"

"There will never be anything more for us. As I have told you on several occasions. You are someone that I regrettably made into my child. Nothing more." He turned to glance at her. "Would that I could do it over I would have simply fucked you and killed you instead of now having to listen to you daily. Do you not have somewhere else you can go?"

Her sputtering made him smile. She was very predictable. He stood there not looking at her, thinking that if she did one more thing to someone in his household, even though he really did not care, he would stake her to the ground and watch with joy her demise. His staff, while small, did not appreciate her ordering them around and telling them that she was soon to be their mistress.

"My lord, I have come to tell you that I think Leon has been duping you. And not only that, but he is stealing some of your most prized possessions. I think that he has several paintings missing from the hallway, and Leon is the only one that has a locked door." He turned to look at her as she continued. "I was going to check to see if they were in his room. I was not…I have seen it many times before in my life as a human and—"

"No doubt you have. Thieves and dopers. What else have you encountered, I wonder, that has made you so…distrustful." Roy moved to his chair and sat. "Go on. You don't want to leave me in suspense now, do you?"

The simpleton smiled at him and sat in the chair. He did not bother pointing out to her that he had given her no leave to do so but watched her primp. He was going to do it today, now, if she did not get to the fucking point.

"He has been leaving the mansion. Daily. For all we know, he has been pinching the pictures there and hording money for later. And the servants, sir. They are not up to what they should be. I believe that Chris will be better served if you put me in charge of the house and give Leon his walking papers. He's a problem for me…you, sir." He waited for her to continue. "I would do a good job for you both. It would be my pleasure after all that you've done for me."

"Let's go over what you've brought me one thing at a time. So you think Leon is leaving daily. I see. And where is it he goes? Do you suppose that he might be…I do not know, going on errands for me? Or do you suppose that he goes to the market to pick up things for the others in the house? You, for instance. I believe that just yesterday you had him pick up some magazine that you had to have. Or is he 'pinching,' as you called it, my household items?"

She shifted on her chair. "I wanted the magazine because it had an article in it that was said to please your man. I only wanted it to see how to make our lovemaking better."

"We do not make love, slave. I fuck you, nothing more. If you get off, then you are welcome, but we in no way, shape, or form make love." He eyed her critically. "You have spent a fortune on dresses. I have the accounting sent to me daily. Who do you suppose picks those up for you if not Leon?"

"I want to please you. I want nothing more than to make you happy and—"

"It would make me happy if I didn't have to see your face until I sent for you. And if I didn't have use for your mouth on my cock, I would have a bag put over your head." He stood up and moved to the window again. "You are one mistake and if I have any more talks with you such as this one, I will take care of you in much the same manner as I did Oscar. You will meet the sun. This meeting is over."

She sat there for several seconds before she stood up. When she was near the door, she stopped. Roy closed his eyes, hoping for her sake that she simply left and didn't return. But he was not that lucky.

"And what of us? Will there never be anything between us? I have given you everything, including my sister, dear. You'll now throw me to the wolves that you stave to get rid of unwanted guest?" He turned to her, his eyes red with anger, his voice hard with it as well.

"There is no 'us.' There will never be an 'us.' And the sister that you have given me? I have not even met her and know that she is ten times, nay, a hundred times, the woman you will ever hope to be. But I ask you this. Where is she? Do you see her now draped over me in sated bliss? And as for the dear sister reference? You did not even have a clear picture of her in your head, for you're so focused on you that you had not even noticed what a beauty you had before you." He walked to her and was glad that she cowered. "You are nothing to me. And will never again curse me with your presence or I will take you to the wolves myself."

He ripped the gown from her. Stripped her naked and then slapped her. When she tried to stand, he pressed his foot to her throat and held her there as he looked down on her.

"Come near me once, slave, and I will take great joy in turning you to dust. Do you understand me?" She nodded. "And you will never speak to or look at Leon again. He is a loyal servant that I won't have you insult again."

He let her up and watched her stagger to the door. Tears stained her face and mingled with the blood from her mouth. She tore down the hall, screaming and sobbing. Roy sat in the chair that was nearby and only looked up when he heard someone there.

"Sir?" He looked at Leon and then at the window. "Is there something amiss? I heard Miss Millicent in her cell. She is very…distraught."

Roy laughed. It was bitter, even to his ears. But he did feel better. He wished that he had done this weeks ago. Finally put the woman in her place. He looked at Leon as he picked up the mess he'd made with her dress.

"She is not to be brought to my chamber again. Clothes will be given to her that would suit her position as a slave, not an honored guest. And if she talks to you, even to ask you the time, I wish to know immediately. I am finished with her lying, bitchy ways." Leon nodded. "What have you for me?"

"The woman you seek is staying on the alpha's compound. I do not know what her relationship with them is. Her house in Virginia is still empty of anyone going in or out." He tied the burden in his hands with a hard yank and tossed it into the trashcan he'd picked up. "I have tried to contact her boss at the police station again. He is out on a vacation. I know not where, and the few officers that I spoke to did not know either. I believe he is out of the country."

Roy nodded. "And the key to the postal box? Have you been able to locate that? Was there any information on who emptied it?"

"Nothing on who might have emptied it. I did manage to locate the one that Oscar had in his possession when he was...when he left us." He laid it on the desk. "The post mistress said that there are two keys, so someone has the other. Have you asked Miss...slave what she has done with hers?"

Roy hadn't realized there were two keys. He tried to remember if anyone had given him the extra and knew that they hadn't. He studied the key on the desk and looked up at Leon.

"Search her cell. I want you to bring me whatever is in the room. Her clothes, any jewelry or personal items as well." Leon said that he would. "And Leon? I want you to make an example of her. I want the room cleaned out thoroughly. Cleaned with the hoses we use to empty the cells when there has been an accident."

Leon smiled. "I will carry out your wishes to the letter sir. There will not be a speck of dust left when I have finished. Would you like for me to make sure that the slave is cleaned as well?"

"Yes." Roy thought he might like to watch this. "Yes. But let me know when you begin. I would like very much to be in on the entertainment of that. It might be the best bit of fun I have had since the unfortunate night that I changed her."

CHAPTER 12

Myles was in the kitchen when Chris came down. He had only meant to go out and get the newspaper before rejoining her in bed. But he'd been waylaid. Myles was very afraid for her.

"You might want to sit down." She did and looked at him. "You remember last night when someone came to the door?"

"Yes. It was late and... Just tell me. Did something happen?" He nodded toward the envelope on the counter. "Have you opened it?"

"No. I did make sure there wasn't anything in it other than a sheet or two of paper. I was worried someone might be sending you something poisonous, but there isn't anything." He picked it up and laid it before her. "It's addressed to you. To Christina Kramer."

He'd wanted to open it. Tear it open and see what this person had to say. Mostly to find out how they knew that she was his mate. He sat a glass of iced water in front of her and then sat across from her. She still hadn't touched the envelope, but did stare at it intently.

"I don't recognize the handwriting. And the envelope looks to be very old, yellowed with age, wouldn't you say? And other than my name on the front, and without checking the back, it looks like it was hand delivered. It came last night. When the person knocked on the door." He'd forgotten that first and foremost she was a detective. "I wonder if it's been sealed with saliva."

"No. There's a wax seal on it. I've taken a picture of it in the event that it gets broken when you open it." He took out his phone and showed her all the pictures he'd taken and told her that he'd emailed them to his account to have them printed. "I've taken a few pictures of the handwriting as well. It doesn't look like the handwriting on the letter from your sister, nor do I think it's the same type of envelope. This is plain where the other was floral."

Picking it up, she brought it to her nose. He knew that she wouldn't smell anything other than maybe the agedness of it. She ran her fingernail under the wax and carefully opened it, keeping the red waxed seal intact. Pouring out the letter rather than pulling it out she dumped it on the table. He handed her a pair of latex gloves. She smiled her thanks.

Opening it just as carefully, she spread it out on the table. It was only one sheet, and he stood up to read it with her. The date at the top was the day before. The signature at the bottom was Leon Bird, in a bold English script.

"Ms. Kramer, I am not a person you will be familiar with, though I do believe you may have found some information about me. You were always very brilliant. My name is, for purposes of this conversation, Leon S. Bird.

"A vampire of great age and power is looking to bring you to his bed. I am sorry for the blandness of the information, but time is of the essence. He will do everything in his power to make this happen. His birth name is Thomas Lyons. His parents were, as they died long ago, full-blooded vampires.

"I have been in his service for nearly three decades but have only just become more to him in the last several weeks. I have been circumventing some of his actions, but he is growing impatient and will, I have no doubt, seek you out sooner than I had planned.

"A woman you know, Millicent Newman, has been helping him. She is a vain, conniving woman who has finally shown her true colors and has been put into her place. I believe that her time here is coming to a close and, if you have any feelings for her, which I cannot see that you have, you may wish to make some arrangements and have her brought to you. I can, for you only, see to it if that is your desire.

"His Lordship has a weakness. He has an unnatural fear of wolves. That is why I have surrounded the mansion with them and keep them starved. He does not know that only I control them. And as such, I wish for you to give the alpha the means in which to do so as well. They will only listen to commands that begin with the word 'love,' a word that his Lordship is not familiar with.

"If all goes well I should like to visit you for a time after this is completed and you kill him for all mankind. I know that your mate is a vampire, but I know little about him. I do hope that he is caring for you in a manner in which you were born to be treated.

"Sincerely, Leon.

"Post Script. I would think that you should contact a Guthrie Calvin in the Department of Supernaturals. Your friend, Holly Campbell, will know of whom I speak."

Myles sat down. He wasn't sure what to think or, for that matter, what to believe in the letter. Chris folded it up and put it back into the envelope before taking off the gloves. When

Chris stood to throw them away, he started to ask her if she was all right. But she spoke first.

"He knows me. And for some time. He is acquainted with Millie and seems to have a true picture of her. Then he says that I am to kill the vampire, like I know what the fuck that is supposed to entail." Myles nodded. "How much of that do you think is bullshit, and how much of it is real?"

"Honestly? I have no idea. Not even about your sister. But if even half of what he says is true, we have more now than we did before." He looked back at the letter. "Would you like to share this with the others?"

"Yes. But Holly first. And Phil." She looked at him with a frown. "Have you ever heard of the department he mentioned?"

He hadn't. He wondered now if it was something that Holly was in charge of. She'd been promoted just after becoming Phil's mate and he realized that he had no idea what that had entailed. He told Chris.

"Contact them. I know that there isn't any way to keep them from talking to each other, but could you ask them to keep this quiet until we talk to them? I don't think anyone here is in on this, but I want to get it in pieces rather than all at once right now. I'm a tad overwhelmed."

He was as well. He reached for Phil and asked him to come to the house as soon as possible and to bring Holly. He did as Chris had asked and told him not to tell the family yet, as it was important. They both arrived a few minutes later.

~~~

Austin read the letter twice. He wasn't thrilled about finding out last, but he could see that Chris was stressed. Myles had taken him aside just after he'd arrived and told him to go easy on her. He told him that not only had Holly confirmed that the department was real, but that she was in charge of the entire unit. She had not, however, been aware that anyone had been put in charge of the case that Leon was in on.

"Chris is having a hard time with this. She said that she's missing something important and is afraid she's leading you guys down a merry path of doom." Austin could see now that she was stressed, but he also thought that babying her wasn't going to get her out of her funk. The woman was much like him, it was either all or nothing with her. He decided to poke the bear and piss her off. Hopefully she didn't kick his ass while she was at it.

"You kept this information from us to make yourself a hero?" She looked at him, then away. "I take it from your lack of an answer that I'm right. That's a really shitty way to repay the people who have been helping you out from the very beginning."

"Austin, you should—" He cut Myles off and nodded to CJ.

"Take him in the other room. I'll have a conversation with him next. This is between the two of us now." To CJ he told her to explain to Myles that he wasn't going to harm Chris but only wanted to piss her off.

"You want to explain to me how this man knows you and seems to think you're some sort of goddess that we need to be bowing before you? Or better yet, how now he's willing to help you after things are going to get out of control?" He stood up. "You seem to have an ally in this jerk. The only conclusion I can see is that you've been playing us."

"You read that in there, dog-boy? Show me." She pulled the copy of the letter from him and scanned it. "Nope. All I see is that he gave you control to a bunch of starving wolves that you couldn't control before. And that he does mention that I don't know him. Or is that his way of throwing you off the track by lying to you. I don't fucking lie, you mother fucking ass hole."

"So you say, and I had no reason to control the wolves before. They weren't on my property, nor were they bothering me. And how do you know that I can control them? Is this another ploy of yours to get me killed?"

He didn't see her move. He had a split second to realize she was stronger and faster since becoming Myles's mate. He didn't even look at the door when someone opened it, so focused he was on saving his own ass.

She had taken him to the floor, chair and all. His ankles were tangled in the legs, and his arms and hands were trapped beneath his body. He didn't know how she'd done it, but he was impressed. The knife at his throat, pure silver, was cutting deep but had not yet broken the skin. He couldn't even shift without her taking off his head.

Her face came close to his, close enough that he could see each eyelash every time she blinked. He watched as her eyes changed from the purple they'd been to the silver of a wolf then the red of a vampire. Christ. She was a shifter.

"Chris, let him up or I'll kill Myles." Austin reached for CJ to tell her "no," but it was too late. Chris charged her before he could move.

"Don't say anything. Anyone. She's not here," Austin said as he stood up slowly and went to his mate. She wasn't hurt, but she was in a position similar to the one he'd been in. Her body pressed against the table and a blade at her throat.

"Christina, let her go. She's not harmed, Myles. See?" Austin nodded to Myles to come toward him. "Look at your mate, Christina. He's unharmed."

Chris came back to herself slowly. First her breathing slowed, then her heart rate began to slow as well. When she stepped back from CJ, Austin told his mate to stay still so as not to spook her again. CJ nodded.

Myles moved to her and stood in front of her so that he blocked the room. As soon as her arms went around him Chris went limp. Myles caught her before she touched the floor. He looked at Austin.

"What the fuck just happened?" Anger surged from Myles, and Austin couldn't blame him. "You pissed her off on purpose, then you wonder why she attacked you? How stupid do you have to be?"

"She isn't human." That had Myles's mouth snap closed. "I don't know what triggered her ability, unless it was anger. But she's a shifter."

Phil came into the room from the office and looked at them all. "She's going to be all right. And you're right Austin, she is a shifter but why she comes forth now I don't... When you put her to bed, Myles, bring me the original letter. Something in it brought her to this point."

"No. I'm going to hold her if it's all the same to you. You want the letter, it's on the desk under the blotter. It's in the envelope. I would say to be careful with it, but I'm reasonably sure that you know to do that." Phil nodded and walked away as Myles looked at him with a great deal less anger. "You knew what she was before?"

Austin shook his head. "Not until she was fighting to shift when she had me down. She's never done that before, I take it?"

"No." Myles pulled her tighter to his chest. "Never. Why didn't I taste it in her blood? Or for that matter..." Myles looked up at him.

"What? You just figured something out. What it is?" Austin looked at Phil when he walked in with the letter. "Tell us both."

"She bit me. When we had sex, she bit me every time. I never thought of it before now. And yesterday..." He looked down at Chris as he continued. "Yesterday when we were finished having...after sex, she drank from me like she was starved."

"This man, Leon, knew what she was and gave her the key to open it in her." Phil sat the letter down and wiped his hand over it, and Austin watched as the letters unscrambled and reformed. "She would have been taught this code early in her life or maybe it was imprinted on her before birth. It's hard to know. I would think that his name here at the end of the sentence was all she had to see. It's the only thing that doesn't change or disappear."

Austin didn't know the language, and it seemed neither did Myles, but Phil did. He read it to them in the language it was written before translating it. *"Time is here. Time knows no enemy. Time to be."* He said that it was a code as old as the first vampires.

"She's a shifter." Myles looked at Phil as he spoke softly. "How did we not know that? How could I have drank from her and not known that?"

"You weren't meant to. She was in hiding and Leon knew it. He triggered her to become what she is for some reason and I doubt very much that even her sister knows." Phil looked over the sheet again. "He said his name is Leon for the purposes of this letter. Do you suppose that he is in hiding, as well?"

"What better place to hide than in front of the nose that seeks you." Austin watched Chris as she sat up on Myles's lap. "You all right?"

"Yes. Are you?" She shrugged and looked at CJ. "I'm sorry. I meant you no harm. I didn't want you to hurt Myles."

"No harm done. You frightened me a little…okay, you scared the shit out of me, but you were protecting what was yours. I can't blame you for that." CJ put out her hand. "Friends?"

Chris nodded and took her hand. She looked over at Austin, then at Phil. She looked so sad that Austin wanted to tell her things would be all right.

"Leon Bird is my uncle. I'm not sure how far back, but he is in there somewhere. He's been waiting for me…watching for me, I suppose, for generations. He thought he was my father, but he only carried the DNA to spawn me. He watched over me until he was called into service by Thomas Lyons, as his father had been before him."

"I've found all I can on the…" Holly looked around the room. "What's happened? Did I miss something?"

Phil brought his mate up to speed, and Myles and Chris started pulling things out of the cabinets and freezer to cook. When first CJ joined them, then Holly, Austin stood to help too. Breakfast was going to be a large affair.

There was tension between the couple. Mostly it came from Chris, but Myles was upset as well. Austin started to tease them but remembered that he'd had his ass handed to him once already today and decided to keep his mouth shut. Holly talked about the department.

"I have a group of men and women working for me that are, for the most part, vampires. There is a mixture of others in the offices, but few. Wolves come in second, but not a good majority of them. Guthrie does have a Leon on his books as an informant. He's been giving them information on the wanted vampire Gates for a few months now. About the time that Peter Newman killed himself. But none of them know what he is and have just assumed he's a smaller, lesser vampire."

"Why isn't he turning him in? What's he waiting for?" Chris put bacon in the pan she was using as she asked. "And why did he wake this thing in me now? Why didn't he do it when this shit first went down?"

"He wants you to kill him." Everyone looked at Myles. "He does. He said so in the letter. If they take him into custody, which is what I'm assuming they'll do, what will they do to him?"

Holly answered him. "They'll try to experiment on him. Try to take a bit of his DNA to see what makes him live so long. Eventually, they'll put him into a cell and leave him there until someone remembers he's there and goes back to conducting all sorts of things on him."

"He'll escape." Austin agreed with Chris on that. "He'll get out and start over. He'll be angrier this time and won't have someone like me around to maybe destroy him."

"So, what is it you want us to do?" Austin moved the eggs to the platter he was using and broke more into the skillet. "You have a plan, right? Tell us what it is so we can end this sucker and move on with our lives."

"You can't help me. If you do, then…what if you get hurt or killed?" She looked at them all, then at Myles. "I can't let anything happen to you. You're all I've ever wanted, and I can't see you hurt."

"I'm going with you, and you won't be able to stop me." He pulled her into his arms, and Austin thought maybe they might make it after all. "You mean just as much to me. What if he hurts you and I'm not there to kick your ass and make you get up to get going again? Who am I going to hide behind when he comes after me?"

"This isn't funny, Myles. You could be killed. You know as well as I do that you didn't sign on for what I am when you bonded with me. I'm nothing like—"

"No, you're not. None of us are. And, until this is finished, none of us ever will be." Austin looked at Myles before he pulled Chris into his arms. "You are a powerful being. You kicked our assess without breaking a sweat. I want to…hell, girl, I need to see you in action that doesn't involve me getting tossed around like a young pup."

She laughed as he'd hoped she would. She straightened up and looked at him. He could see the fire beginning to burn in her eyes. He smiled at her.

"If you get your ass kicked by this guy, don't come whining to me. I'll have enough on my plate trying to save your ass." She looked at CJ. "You okay with this too, bitch?"

"It's 'alpha person' thank you very much, and yes, I am. I'm ready for some major showdown." CJ smiled. "Now, get away from my mate before I get pissy with you. You go and hug your own. Mine is not for you."

Breakfast was served with a great deal of talk and planning there, as well. Austin laughed when Phil teased Myles about his house finally looking good, and Chris told him that he was welcome in the guest room any time hell froze over. By the time the dishes were done they had a plan. A good plan, not a great one, but he'd moved on less. In just a few hours they were going to storm the castle.

CHAPTER 13

"Leon." He cringed when his name was bellowed like that. He turned to go toward the man he hated more than anything he could think of. He smiled as he entered the bed chamber. Leon spared a glance at the woman on the floor with very little compassion.

"Yes, sir." Leon nodded to him as a show of respect, but had none. He looked up when nothing else was forthcoming.

"She said you opened the postal box." Leon glanced at the woman and then at Roy. "She said that the reason you had this key was because you had the second one and that she never saw it."

Leon nodded and walked to the file cabinet he'd set up several weeks before. He'd been anticipating this move and had gone to great pains to cover his tracks. He opened the second drawer and pulled out a file. Taking out the paperwork, he handed it to him and stepped back.

"Is that not her signature? And the handwriting that is scrawled at the top, is that not hers?" Leon waited while Roy looked. When Roy searched for something on his desk, Leon was glad now that he'd planted the paper with her handwriting.

157

The woman simply had to go. She was causing too much in the way of problems for him and, as he had no way of knowing if the young miss cared for her or not, he was going to ask her forgiveness rather than wait on permission.

Roy laid them both down after a few minutes and told her to stand. "Slave, the evidence is here to view if you wish. But I believe even a fool could tell that the handwriting is the same. And though I have told you...threatened you harshly not to come to my chamber again, here you—"

"He forged my name." Millicent looked wildly around the room. "Let me show you my handwriting now and compare it. I'll prove to you that I had nothing to do with that fucking post box but to tell him to open it."

Roy looked at him, then at the woman. Leon had known that she'd bury herself sooner or later and was sad she chose now to do so. He had planned to use her as a distraction when the time came. Leon wasn't going to try and keep her from her death, but he was sad that it happened now.

"So you think if I were to let you write something, I would see a difference?" She nodded and smiled at him. "You would in no way change your handwriting so that I would see a difference, would you, slave?"

"No." She licked her lips, a sure sign she was lying. "I wouldn't do that. I would...well, that would be cheating wouldn't it?"

Leon didn't say anything when Roy looked at him. He didn't think she needed any more help to get herself killed. Roy laughed slightly. Even from where he was standing, Leon could see that the man was on edge. Anger seemed to vibrate from him and fill the room.

"Of course it will be." He got up and went to a box in the corner. "The other day when we cleaned your room, do you know what we found?"

She shivered and glared at him. Leon waved at her and blew her a kiss. He'd had a great deal of fun that day. Using the large hose to spray down the room first, then her body, had been something that he had enjoyed immensely.

Her skin hadn't fared well under the massive water pressure and her nude body had been torn to shreds. And Roy had had a chair brought down to the sublevels to watch her humiliation. Both of them had had a good laugh during and after the ordeal. The box was a result of the search. And Leon hadn't needed to plant any of it.

Roy pulled out the ruined cell phone. A small iPad, as well as a charger for both pieces, was taken out next as well as a limp notepad. In it were credit card numbers, passwords, and the combination to the safe in this room and the one in his bedchamber. Also, there was a large dildo and some other sex toys.

"You had a great deal of fun at my expense, it seems." He looked at Leon. "Did you order these for her, or did you use them with her?"

There was humor there, but Leon was so mortified by the thought that he would touch one such as her, he stiffened and told him no.

"I did not think so." He looked at Millicent. "So you ordered these things as well as used monies not given to you by me to purchase them. Is that about right?"

"I had needs that weren't being met." She flushed and lowered her tone. "I needed you, but you did not seem to need me. I was lonely and thought to prepare myself for you."

Leon thought the exact words that Roy said. "Sure you did." Roy put everything back into the box and handed it to her. She looked pleased, but Leon had an idea she wouldn't be much longer. He'd been given an order earlier this evening.

"Leon. Her needs need to be met. Would you please take her to the bedchamber now and make sure that she is prepared?" Leon nodded and moved to carry her box. "No, she'll need those as well."

"Thank you, my lord. I'll please you in ways that you won't want anyone else in your bed. I will be the best fuck you've ever had." He smiled as she continued. "Will you be joining me soon?"

"Never." Her face registered shock as Roy continued. "Take that away from me and let me know when it is finished."

Leon walked out the door and had the two men there bring her along. She was cooperating for a few feet until she looked where he was taking her. She knew how this was going to end, it seemed. The fighting began, but it was much too late and the men with him were much stronger than she was. He dragged her into the large chamber and had her chained to the posts above her head and stripped of her clothing. When she was naked, he dismissed the men with a nod. Then he walked as close to the slave as he could without actually touching her.

"You might have been better off simply doing as the rest and laid low instead of trying to play a game you had no way of winning." He walked around to face her. "Your tears mean nothing to me, nor does your pleading."

A gag was placed in her mouth; the large ball prevented her from doing anything more than breathe around it. Leon went to the door that had been hidden behind a large curtain and knocked once. He stood watching her face as the first man came up behind her. He was hard and thick. His cock took her ass hard, and she screamed around the gag.

"Does it feel as if you prepared yourself enough, slave? Does his cock leave you wanting for more?" The man behind her slammed into her over and over while he held her still.

When he grunted his climax, he stepped back. Another man took his place.

Leon watched her as four more men took her. Each of them taking her ass hard over and over without mercy. When she fainted, he simply brought her around with water and waited for her to look at him. He wanted to watch her as she was punished.

She was hanging limply now, and Leon nodded again to the man still standing as a statue near another door. When he nodded back, he opened the door and let the first of many men in.

"You might find these men more to your liking. They will take your pussy. I'm not sure that any of them won't feed on you. They had asked and I told them whatever they wanted. If you have an objection, please say so."

The first man was as large as the other man, only his dick was longer. When he ripped her head up, he slammed his cock into her and his fangs deep into her throat. Leon was aroused at the suffering she endured, not the coupling. When this man finished, two more came from the room, each taking much from her vein as they emptied inside of her. Leon walked up to her when they finished.

"I want you to know before your last punishment comes to you that I did everything you said I did. I did set up the postal box, I did have the extra key. I even fed the master information for him to watch you and your spending of his funds." He walked all the way around her and saw the blood pour down her thighs. "I would have kept you around just a little longer, long enough for you to see him die by the hand of another, but you went too far too soon."

She closed her eyes again, and he slapped her. When she looked at him, hatred was there, as well as the pain. He wanted her to hate him. Her pain was secondary to what he needed from her. Leaning into her throat, he licked her pulse. It was slow and faint under his tongue. He bit her hard, tearing at the flesh there.

"That will be for the wolves. They love a good, bloodied meal." Her screaming made him smile, and he ordered her let down. As he dragged her to the doors to the yard, he whistled sharply and watched his pets come toward him.

They were thin and starving. He hadn't fed them properly in a few weeks. He noticed, too, that three were missing. They had started eating each other. Good. Less for him to poison later if they became a problem. He shoved her toward them. She tried to struggle back, but the first of them, the larger of the wolves, caught her leg. She was being dragged back when he reached out to her and took off the gag.

"I want him to hear you scream. I want all of them to hear you suffer." He pushed her forehead back. "You will bother me no more."

He watched them pounce on her. Her limbs were torn into, her face bitten open. He knew that as a vampire she would heal somewhat, but not as quickly as they could feast on her. When the arm that had been ripped from her body was being taken away by two of the smaller wolves, he smiled. Soon she would be nothing but broken bones, all her flesh gone into their bellies. He looked up at the balcony when he heard a door close. He would have had to see that his wishes were carried out. He might be afraid of the wolves, but he had to respect their ability to get the job done.

Leon waited until she was gone. Only a few pieces of her remained and those were being fought over by the younger, weaker wolves. After walking into the mansion, he closed the door and tried to hide his smile. She was gone, he didn't have to worry that she would catch him any longer. Knocking on the door to the master bedchamber, he was glad now that he'd never pledged to the man. He was able to move freely without fear of being found out.

"She is no more, my lord. I have made sure that what we had discussed was carried out and that she was disposed of."

The master didn't move from the window. Why he stood there was beyond Leon. He could not see out, as it had been covered over many years ago. All that he could see was his own reflection and nothing more. But the man was mad, completely and totally insane.

"Find Christina. I want her here tonight and in my bed when I wake." Leon nodded. "If you fail me on this, Leon, I will feed you to those wolves myself."

"Yes, sir. Tonight."

Leon went out of the chamber and down to the sublevels. He had to warn her and now it was imperative that he leave, too. When he was as far into the levels as they went, he looked around. No one had been this way in centuries before his father had told him where they were. He reached up into the crevice and pressed the small button. When the wall behind him slid open he moved into the dank hall and waited for it to close. Soon, he was moving toward the outside and freedom.

He pulled out the cell phone that he'd hidden there. He'd had to move quickly and he was weak from relief that it was finally coming to an end. After pressing the button to call the only number on this phone, he waited. He hoped that someone would answer. A small child did.

"I would very much appreciate it if I may speak to your alpha, please. He is…who is this?" The young person giggled, and Leon was afraid that he'd lost. When someone spoke again, he nearly laughed with relief.

"I am Leon Bird. I would like to get a message to Christina Kramer, please. Tell her today. It must be today." The woman tried to get him to wait so that she could write it down, but he told her again. "Tonight. All is ready for tonight."

He hung up the phone and took out the battery. Then he broke the phone into pieces. He had had to work very hard at getting the alpha's phone number and hoped that no one had changed it. He moved further into the woods and to the cave his father had shown him so many decades ago. He moved deeper into it and to where he'd stored so much.

Every trash can he'd emptied from the office had been marked and dated in a box. Every piece of clothing that had been taken from someone, every driver's license, every piece of ID he'd been able to find and save was in here. And there were things for the young miss as well.

Money galore. Jewels and gems that he'd been able to pocket or had carried out and brought here. Paintings that had, at one time, graced the walls of large museums and art galleries that Roy had stolen and had not even missed when they'd been taken away from him. Bolts of material from centuries gone by preserved and kept clean and dry by him and his father and his father before him. Payments, decades and decades of payments for the girl who would free so many by killing a man so evil that he had been named for the very act. They had waited for so long for her that many had despaired of her ever coming for them. But not Leon.

Leon had been the first to find her seed in the man who would sire her. Leon had been the one to plant the information into the womb she would grow in. Information on what she was, what she had to do, and most importantly, on the man she had to kill. He had prepared her for what was to come and to make sure that above all else she was kept safe.

Leon knew that he'd nearly lost her once. It was when a man who had been sent by the others to find and destroy her. Someone had found out who she'd been. The man had found her when she'd been moving people out of a fire and the warehouse was nearly ready to go. Leon had heard what was happening to her well after she'd been shot already. Going to her, he'd been able to push her, give her the extra strength needed to kill the man. Leon had, of course, destroyed the man's body. No questions were ever asked about him or why he had acted as he had. The man was a shifter, as she was.

Leon made his way to the home where she was. He had to make sure that she was prepared and that she would know what was needed of her. He could answer questions for her so long as she did what they needed. As he got closer to the house, he could smell her clean spirit. But he missed the scent of the large wolf behind him.

The low growl was loud in the quiet morning. Leon turned slowly, making sure that he did not startle the were. He knew that this one was not the same as before. This one as bigger, meaner, and was the alpha. Leon dropped before the man and bowed his head low.

"I mean you and yours no harm. I come to help the young miss. She is my master and has been for many years." The wolf snarled at him and moved closer. "You're Force, the alpha. I am Leon Bird."

The wolf moved toward him. Leon didn't move. Fear had him remaining as still as stone. He thought he was being herded and stood up. He told the wolf he would go where he needed him to, but he must see his master. Leon smelled her before he saw her.

"He wants to know what you are." Chris spoke softly, but he had no problem hearing her, nor had the wolf either, it seemed. His snarl made Leon believe that she was not listening to his commands.

"I am Leon Bird. I am your servant." She looked around, and that's when Leon noticed the pack surrounding him. "Miss?"

"He didn't ask you who you were, but what. You're not a wolf, and you most certainly aren't a vampire. You aren't like me, either. What the fuck are you?"

He bowed before her, dropping to his knees and pressing his nose to the earth. He looked up at her, barely raising his face, and told her.

"I am whatever you need me to be."

CHAPTER 14

Chris sat and stared at the man as each of the others in the room shouted questions at him. He had answered them all with the exception of how he'd come to find her and what he was doing here now. She knew he would for her, would have to answer her, but she wasn't sure yet she wanted to know the answers. She looked at Myles when he sat next to her.

"I am her mate, Myles Kramer. You know who I am?" Leon nodded and smiled. "Do you have to treat me, her mate, with the same code of honor that you give to her?"

"I do. Though you should know, master, that my first loyalty is to her now and forever and I will only do as she bid me even if it is to kill you. It is my duty to keep her from harm in any way." Myles nodded and looked at her.

"So, my mate is your responsibility, correct?" Leon nodded and Chris could see a little respect come to Leon's eyes. "So if I were to tell you to kill…say anyone in this room, you'd have to do it."

"If it is your desire, yes. But if she tells me not, then I will not go against her." Leon looked around the room. "But you will not order me to do so. These people are your friends, family almost. To have me kill them would not be in your nature."

Austin laughed. "Thank God. I was getting a little worried there, Myles. If he's to do whatever you need of him, then order him to kill the prick that's trying to get her."

"I cannot and she knows this." Chris looked at Austin and told him that Leon was right. "She is aware of a great many things she did not know before. Her mind had been unlocked now."

Chris stood up and took Leon's hand. He let her, and when he pulled up his sleeve, she found just what she thought she would. A mark. It was like the one she'd found on her own arm earlier. One that had appeared on Myles's arm, too, just after they'd gotten up this morning, about the time the call had come from Austin that someone had called his house.

"What is this? And why is it just now showing up on me?" She pulled her sleeve up higher and pointed to the second one that neither man had. "And what is this one?"

Before he touched her, he asked for her permission. Then he looked to Myles. She thought it funny that he'd asked for permission when everything around them seemed so surreal.

"This is the mark of your kind. I carry it as well as your mate because he is as you are now. Any children you have will also carry the mark until such time that you may have to go into hiding again. Then it will hide on your skin until one such as me would unlock it." He didn't touch the one higher but seemed to hover over it slightly. "This is not a mark I have unlocked. It was there before but hidden until the time was right. It is the mark of your birth."

"And that means what? That I was born? I got that." She knew it was much more when he shook his head. "I don't think I want to know what it is or what it means."

"As you wish." He sat up straighter in the chair. "But you will need to show it to his Lordship before you kill him. It will mean a great deal to him."

She stood up and began to pace. She looked at Phil and Myles as they sat quietly and then over at Austin and CJ. The others had been asked to patrol the grounds, and she knew that Austin was keeping them updated on what was going on in here. She looked over at Mr. and Mrs. Campbell, Phil's parents. They hadn't said a word since they'd arrived.

"You know, don't you?" Hope nodded, but her husband shook his head. "What he's saying, is it true?"

"Yes. He hasn't lied to you once, neither by omission nor by words. He can't lie to you or to Myles. He is your servant, like he said. He is a rare breed in that he will serve you until his death. And there is something else you should know, you cannot die." She turned to look at Myles. "Nor can he. But you should let him tell you what you are. I believe it to be very import—"

Leon stood up. "He knows that I am here. He cannot leave because of the wolves, but he is very angry."

"Can he harm you while you're here?" He shook his head, then nodded. "Which is it, buddy? I can't protect what I don't understand."

"You would protect me?" Leon dropped to his knees again and looked up at her. "He cannot harm me from where he is, but he can if he comes here. He will not just destroy what he sees but things he cannot. Nothing will live if it touches it. No roots, nor any living thing, will survive his anger if he leaves the grounds. You must go to him now."

She looked around the room and started to tell them this was her fight, but the words died on her lips. All of them were dressed for battle. Those that could shift had, and the ones that could not were in armor. Phil took a step forward as his shield lifted.

"There are nine hundred vampires on standby. There are a great many more wolves both were and natural. We will go with you to fight beside you." She looked at Myles.

"I thought I'd stay here and bake a few dozen cookies while you were gone." The only person who didn't laugh was Leon. "I'm kidding her. I'm going with her to keep her out of trouble if I can. I don't think it'll work, but I'm still going to give it a try."

Chris walked to him and crushed her mouth over his. She wanted to have him hold her, but she, too, could feel Roy's anger. They moved as one to the yard. She was nearly overwhelmed by the show of force. She moved toward the tunnels where Leon told her to enter. She knew that all of them were following her. She looked up to see Leon standing next to her.

"You can't go." He looked at her, crestfallen. "I need you protected. You said yourself that he could harm you. I can't let you be hurt. I need you. My children will need you. You must remain safe for them."

"My lady, there is…" He nodded and handed a blade to her. "When you reach the end of the tunnel, let the alpha go first. He will need to control the wolves on the grounds. He can control them for any reason, do you understand me?"

"Yes. He can make them fight for me instead of against me." Leon nodded at her. "I need you to protect the children. All of them. There are many at the compound, don't let any harm come to them."

"I will not, my lady. I will care for them as I have you." He bowed to her. Then to Myles. "Be quick and safe."

Then he disappeared. Myles came up to her and kissed her mouth. He looked fierce and sexy, and she told him so.

"We'll satisfy your odd sense of timing later. For now, let's go kick some major ass."

Going into the tunnel, she felt the rightness of what they were doing. They were a force. And she knew that she couldn't have done this alone, not and come out victorious.

~~~

Roy knew she was coming, the person he'd been hiding from for nearly a thousand years. He could feel her, knew that she was coming for him and knew that, like those before her, she would fail.

Looking at the wolves roaming just outside his doors he knew a real kind of fear. If he didn't leave now she would find him. If he left, they would tear him apart. He wasn't afraid of the girl. She was a mere flea in his life. Something that he would flick away and move on. But the wolves would keep him from going to his shelter. He summoned for Leon again.

There had been nothing since he'd had him get rid of the slave. He looked at the men he'd called to him. Ten. There were only ten men in service for him and he still had not been able to summon Leon. He knew then that he'd never drank from the man nor had he been pledged to. He'd been a fool. But not any longer.

"Destroy as many of them as you can. I want to see them reduced in number before sunrise." He turned to look at them when they did not move. "You heard me. Go out and kill the wolves that dare block my path."

The men moved, but not quickly enough. When he grabbed the first man up and snapped his neck Roy knew he'd just killed his only hope of getting by the vicious animals below, but it had the desired effect on the men. They left the room, drawing swords as they went.

He felt her the moment she stepped onto his property. Closing his eyes he looked beyond the trees and the hills in his mind's eye. He stretched his vision to come face to face with her and suddenly knew real anger.

"You." It was the girl from the picture. The woman he'd nearly brought into his home and to his bed. The woman that her sister, his slave, had first brought to his attention. So long ago it seemed, a woman of unparalleled beauty was in Millicent's dreams and thoughts. A woman like no other. And he'd been correct, she was like no other.

She had come. She had been born to destroy him and now she was here. Leon had many sins to pay for when he found him. So many that he was looking forward to seeing him. Moving through the household, Roy made his way to the steps of his home and called forth the earth around him. He barely glimpsed the carnage around him where the wolves had killed each man, as none were there in the yard.

"Protect me now." He pushed the earth to move. "Shield this house so that she may not enter."

The wolves started to bay. Roy smiled, not bothering to look what was causing them to be afraid. He knew what the grounds looked like when they did his bidding. It was powerful and destructive. Massive movements that would do as he bid, shelter him and what was his. Roy commanded all because of what he was, he was everything.

The first stir of air touched his face, and he lifted his head to greet it. He'd expected more and lifted his arms high and closed his eyes to the power that was him. When nothing else moved, he opened his eyes and looked beyond.

She stood there in the field, smiling at him less than fifty feet from where he stood. She had no weapon that he could see, nor did she have any army. Others before her had come wearing armor that he stripped from them with a blink of his eye. Swords made by the best blacksmiths with special powers and spells woven into the very fabric of what they were. He'd cut them down with a nod and had disarmed them with a flick of his wrist. He would do more to this woman.

"Hi," Chris said. Roy looked at her as she waved at him. "I've come here to kill you. I know you kinda think that's not possible, but you should know that I'm not your run of the mill girl. I've been kicking ass bigger than yours for years."

Roy laughed and she joined him. "You think to come here and best me on my own grounds? Without weaponry or powers? You must be mad. That is not the half of it. You are quite mad."

"Could be. I've been called a lot worse." She looked around him, and he looked as well. "As for the weaponry, I'm not so sure that I need it. But as you can see, I brought my own army."

Roy stumbled back when they began to walk toward him. Wolves, hundreds of them moved as a unit toward were he stood and sat on their haunches and snarled at him. He knew that they had been joined by his own when one of them snapped their massive mouth at him. But that was not all.

Vampires came too. Thousands of them all dressed in their war gear, old and new. He knew who stood out front beside the man who held the hand of his assassin. He was the Lord of Vampires, Phil Campbell.

He tried to act as if he wasn't afraid but he'd heard tales of him. Also of the man who could command the wolves of any breed. Roy looked to his left, wondering if he should go toward the mountains that were at his back.

"I wouldn't." He looked at her then. "I wouldn't go and do that if I were you. I've been working on this plan, you see, and I've brought all manner of help to carry it out. And even if you try, you can't leave. You're powers have been…" She looked at the man standing next to her, opposite of the Lord. "What happened to his powers?"

"Denuded. He's been rendered incapable of leaving with a trial at hand. He has been stripped off all his powers per rules of the council. They explained this to you before we left, love. Remember?"

She smiled at him, then looked at Roy. "You are hereby on trial. There will be a short trial, then you'll be—"

"You can't do this to me. I'm vampire. I am all of them. They should all bow down before me." His voice thundered across the grounds, and he watched in satisfaction as her hair blew back. "You'll bow before me before this day is through."

She laughed at him. He started across the grounds to her but stopped suddenly when a wolf stepped in front of him. Roy looked at her and she laughed again.

"You know, you're a great big blow hard. You expect that all should worship you simply because you wish it. Not going to happen. Especially with me." She looked around at the masses. "And I would imagine these guys, too. You might be better off just fucking the hell off and going back to where you come from."

"Or what will you do if I do not." He took another step toward her when the wolf moved. "You're nothing to me but a child. A shifter with no purpose. What consequence is it to me if you do not think I should be worshipped? You are nothing."

She moved forward, quick and hard. He refused to back away, and he was not going to show her anything but the contempt that he felt for her and her kind. When she was within touching distance she pulled out her blade. It wasn't until he got a good look at it that he worried. Someone, most likely Leon, had given this to her.

Roy knew the blade. But without the right power, without the right person holding it, it was simply a blade. He grinned at her, showing her his fangs, the length and size of them impressive even to him. She laughed and then looked behind her.

She turned back to him and flipped the bejeweled blade over and over in her hand, catching it every time by the handle and not the silver. When she flipped it up and caught it behind her Roy folded his arms over his chest and tried to look bored.

"You said this was a trial. I have yet to see anything but you playing parlor tricks and playing childish games. I demand that you allow me to go in peace. Give me back my powers and leave this place." He turned to Phil. "You have anything to say? If not, let me go."

"I, Phil Campbell of the Paranormal Council, find you, Thomas Lyons, also known for these proceedings as Roy Gates and any other name that you have gone by, guilty of acts of treason, murder, murder of your own kind, theft of monies of your people, money laundering, drugs and drug paraphernalia sales, prostitution—"

Roy laughed. "You have no proof of this. None. You can make up all the titles you wish to tag me with, but you have no proof."

"You're so right. We don't have shit." The blade in her hand suddenly glowed a blinding white. Roy took a step back and nearly fell. When she ran the sharp end of it into her sleeve and tore it open, he began to wonder if she was her. When she showed him the mark, he knew that he had to get away or die. He looked at her and pretended indifference.

"If you think to frighten me with a mark of a breed I killed out long ago, then go you must. But I will not beg mercy of you or anyone. I would rather be imprisoned than to be put to death by you." He moved forward as she did, and he knocked the blade from her fingers.

He was going to kill her and, once he did, he would come back to fight another day. Centuries from now, when another of her kind came to try and take him down, Roy would be more prepared, more diligent, and he most certainly would be better armed with an army for her. But she did not fall as he had planned; his blade missed its mark when she moved. He cried out in frustration.

Roy watched her flip, her body becoming as fluid as wine. She landed on her hands, then rolled quickly until she was behind him. He glanced to see where her blade had landed and realized it was gone. Before he could move from her to snatch it up and out of her reach she was at his back with the blade at his throat. Roy did not even move to look at her.

"You have fucked up my engagement, you've fucked up my moving into my new home, and you fucked with the wrong chick." The blade sliced across his throat. "And you fucked with my family."

He dropped to his knees and grabbed at his throat. Blood poured from his wound, and he worked hard to repair it. When she stood in front of him, he looked up at her. He knew real fear when he looked deeply into her shifting eyes.

When she leaned forward, he reached for her. He was going to take her with him to hell and that would be it. But he felt the blade enter him again. His chest exploded from the silver tip that pierced him and entered his heart. Pain tore through his body. He was dying. The chit had killed him. When her booted foot came out and touched his forehead he fell backwards and onto the ground. The last thing Roy saw was her laughing face before he incinerated.

CHAPTER 16

Myles watched her walk around the yard. She'd been doing that every day since she'd killed Roy. He started out for her, but Leon stopped him. He asked to speak to him before he spoke to his mistress.

"She is not well, my lord." Myles wanted to tell him "no shit" but kept his answer down to a nod. "She believes that she has failed everyone."

Myles looked at the man. "Why the hell would she think that bullshit? She saved us all. Killed that asshole when no one else could."

"But that does not negate the fact that she feels as if she has failed. Killing the master had not been an easy thing for her. To look a man in the face when you take his life is something so few can do and walk away. Yet there she is. Everyone here knows that she is a killer. She did not let the trial finish though he was sentenced to die long before the field was entered." Leon looked out the window at his mistress. "Her heart is heavy. She will not be well for a very long time, I'm afraid, unless something is done."

"They said she couldn't die." He looked at her and noticed that she'd lost weight and she was pale. "What's wrong with her?"

"As I have said, her heart is heavy. Would you like to hear my opinion?" Leon had been telling them things for days now. "It is one that I believe will help her."

"Tell me. But make it the short version. I'm worried about her." He looked at Leon. "I can't lose her. She's all I have in the world."

"That is not true, my lord. You have a great deal more than her. You have family with the Forces. They have accepted you when you yourself did not." Myles looked at Leon, ready to tell him he was wrong, when the man continued. "Who has come to see her?"

"What? They all have. I had a parade of people coming in and out of here daily until…" He looked at the calendar. "Until this was over."

"Correct, sir. No one has come to see either of you since she killed the master. She has had no one to speak to. You have told her on numerous occasions that you would like to simply forget it, have you not?" Myles nodded. "And when she has asked you about the others, the Forces, you tell her what, my lord?"

"That I'll go and see them. And I do. Without her." He got up to pace. "I've been trying to keep her from having to explain what she did. She seemed to want to forget the entire thing. She was so upset when she returned here that I thought she was too upset."

"You have sheltered her. You have tried to keep her safe." Myles nodded. "She does not need either. She needs to live."

Myles watched her walk back and forth. Leon had said she needed to live. He thought she was, but apparently she'd not been living so much as she'd been simply existing. He reached for his phone and called the one person that he knew would help him.

"Nancy, this is Myles. I need…She's fading from me and I'm terrified I'm going to lose her." Tears streamed down his face as he continued. "She's lost weight and she looks so pale. She's not interested in sex, and I don't think she's slept an entire night in over a week."

"Where is she now?" He told her. "Oh that poor child, that poor child. Her pain is so deep, deeper than I thought it would be. You've left her to her grief too long. We all have."

"Grief? I don't think she cared enough about the man to grieve over him." Myles started to tell her that he thought it was something more.

"Oh son. She lost her only family that day. Not the monster that she killed, but her sister. That is why we have stayed away. She was so hurt by the fact that she'd not been able to save the idea of her family. She needed time to heal from that. Her grief is profound, I would imagine. To have a sister only to wash your hands of her so that her death is on your hands as well. She is grieving for the family, not the sister."

"Yes. Me too. I never…she never said anything. She goes into the yard and walks around and around." Nancy sniffled. "I have to do something. I can't let her fade away like this. She's hurting so badly and—"

"And it hurts you not to be able to fix it." He heard her speaking to someone else, the phone muffled for a minute. "You stay right where you are. I'm coming now. So is…do you have plenty of food? Never mind. I shall come prepared."

She simply hung up, and he did the same. Myles kept an eye on Chris until he heard the first wolf howl. She looked off into the direction. Then she came into the house. He reached for her, but she moved to the sink.

"I thought I'd make some pork chops for dinner. Are you hungry?" He looked at the clock. It was only two in the afternoon.

"Not yet. I made us a salad for lunch. You didn't come in. Are you hungry now?" She shook her head and looked into the refrigerator. "Chris, honey, are you all right?"

"Of course," she said from the depths of the freezer. "I'm just tired. I don't think I'm sleeping all that well. Maybe I should sleep in the guest room for a little while."

He was at the point of saying no when he heard a loud knock at the front door. He stomped in there to tell Nancy that he'd changed his mind. That he was going to have it out with her. But it wasn't Nancy; it was Patrick.

"Hi there. I was wondering if I was...is Chris here?" Myles nodded and pointed to the kitchen. Myles asked if he could handle the large bowl in his hand, and the boy looked at him like he was so stupid. He'd been getting that look from a lot of people lately.

Before he could close the door, he was being pushed out of the way by Nancy and CJ. They were arguing about the type of flour to use...he thought. He started to shut the door.

"There's more in the truck. Bring it in. Oh and show Austin where to take that keg." Myles looked out at the truck and saw the big man rolling a keg off the truck end. He looked back at CJ as she disappeared around the corner.

He walked outside and looked at the back end of the truck. "I only spoke to her twenty minutes ago. How the hell did she organize this so fast?"

Austin shrugged. "She's my mom. How the hell should I know? And for the record, I had nothing to do with you having this keg. Connor asks how your bachelor party keg got here; I'm going to tell him you did it."

Myles nodded, not really understanding. He helped carry the cases of food to the porch and someone else took it in. Before they took the last one off, two more trucks pulled up just as loaded.

"We having a party?" Gordon nodded with a grin. Myles looked at the hamburger and hot dogs in the back of his truck. There were nine coolers of them. He looked at Gordon.

"These are for the kids. The adults are having steaks. Mom called in all sorts of favors, and we were dispatched to pick stuff up. Alexis and Stacy are coming with the kids, and Holly and Lou are bringing the last of the things that we couldn't get."

Phil pulled up next in a sporty car. He got out and walked up to the group of them. Myles looked at the trucks, then at the car. He asked Phil where his was.

"I do not drive trucks. There is nothing wrong with them, but I, myself, don't like them." Laughing and carrying a child in one hand and a case of vegetables in the other, he entered the kitchen, and Myles followed him. The first thing Myles saw was Patrick giving Chris a lesson in something and Nancy watching them fondly.

"You could have told me that we were having a party." He kissed Nancy's cheek as he took the little girl in her arms. "I would have told you to stay away."

She hit him with her spoon. He laughed at her and went to Chris. She was just getting a hug from Patrick who informed him that he was going to see to the fire.

"How did this happen?" He shrugged at her question. "Maybe I should ask you *when* this happened."

"I don't know that either, but if Gordon asks, Austin stole his keg." He grinned at her when she slapped him on the shoulder. "If you want me to, I can tell them all to go home."

"Yeah, like that would work." She looked out the back at the kids. "Patrick is the only one that wasn't adopted to another family."

"That's because I asked that he not be put up for it." She looked at him like she was going to rip into him, then he kissed her. "We're going to take him. If you want to, that is. He already loves you."

"You think...I don't know, Myles. A child around here? He won't...what if..." She looked away from the children playing. "I think he would be better off with a real family."

When she walked outside, he stood here until someone slapped him on the shoulder. He turned to look at Lou. She had a wooden spoon in her hand, as did the rest of the women in the room.

"We can and will beat the crap out of you if you don't go after her." Lou looked at Nancy before she continued. "You have about an hour. Time enough for you to go find her and do whatever manly thing you think you need to and get her back here."

"She might not want me to come—" The spoon in Nancy's hand flashed out and caught him on the forehead. "You're going to miss that one of these days."

"You might too. Now go after the girl before I beat you with it." She lifted it again. "You have an hour. Make it work."

~~~

Chris stepped into the tunnel and took a right instead of going straight. She'd been here so many times in the past week that she could walk along the rough path and not trip. She turned just as Myles entered behind her.

"You've been here before." She nodded. "You come here to get away from me, or just to get away? I've missed you."

"I come here to…to both, I guess. Not so much to get away from you but to give you whatever space you need." She moved farther down the path. "And to look at this."

Myles whistled behind her. "Shit. What is all this? It looks like some of this stuff is really old."

"I think it is. Leon took me here the first day. He said it was my payment for what I'd done." She picked up one of the many gold pieces and handed it to Myles. "He said that many more before me had tried and failed. This was to be their payment, and when nothing became of it, it was held until someone killed him."

She moved along the stacks of framed art, along the large wooden cases of pottery and gold. Chris picked up a small frame and looked at it before moving on. She sat down on a stack of crates.

"And this upsets you." She nodded at Myles. "Why?"

Why? She had been asking herself the same question for days now. Why was she able to kill him when no others had been able to? Why was she supposed to bring all those people with her when she'd been the one to do it? Why had it been important to everyone that they stand behind her? She looked at Myles and asked him.

"Why did you need all those people there? I think that's the real question. Why? Did they need a witness? No, I don't think that's the reason. I believe that everyone would have known if you had failed. Was it because *if* you failed, they could take care of him? Had that been the case, then someone besides you could have killed him long ago. No, you had to do it. I think they were there as your support."

"Support to what? You just said yourself that I was the only one who could kill him. Had I failed, they would have been in harm's way and he would have killed them after he killed my ass." She picked up another coin. "You think that this stuff, all these riches, would have made up for anything if anyone of you would have been harmed? If you had been harmed in any way?"

"No. No I don't. But let me ask you this. Had you not had the people behind you, what would you have done?" She looked at him, not understanding the question. "If we hadn't have been there, what would you have done?"

"I would have done it anyway." He shook his head. "Then I guess I don't understand what you're asking me."

"I'm asking you had you not had us standing beside you and with you, would you have worked so hard to kill him." She started to speak and he stopped her. "We all saw what you did. You kept going toward him to keep him away from the rest of us. The further you were away, you figured the safer we were, didn't you?"

She looked away, embarrassed that he'd seen that. "I thought it was important that he was as far from his prey as he could get. I don't know if that was my plan at all."

He pulled her chin around to face him. He looked into her eyes. She saw his love there and his understanding. She tried to pull away when he held her still.

"You did that because we were there. You saved us not only because you killed the worst man to ever walk the earth, but you saved us from ourselves." He kissed her gently on the mouth. "I love you, Christina."

"I failed her." She waited for him to tell her she had, and when he didn't answer, she continued. "I know that she was the reason for all this. I mean partly, anyway. I keep thinking that had she not agreed to turn me over to him, I wouldn't have been there to do what needed to be done. Was she a pawn in this whole nightmare? Was she slated to die so that I could win?"

"I don't know the answer to that." She stared at the things in the cave around them without seeing them. He sat next to her, and she wanted to ask him…no, beg him, to leave her alone.

"What I do know is that I failed you, too." She jerked around to look at him. "I did. You were so hurt and I didn't do anything about it. I walked around the house waiting for you to tell me how to fix whatever it was that was hurting you without a thought to ask you why. You killed a man that none other, not even me, could have slain for you. You killed a vampire that was thousands of years old and had such great powers that no one, not a single person, could have done either. But you did. And I stupidly thought that you were too strong to let it bother you."

"I killed him because it was my job. I killed him because I—"

"You killed him because you love us." He pulled her into his lap, and she laid her head on his chest. "You do love us. I wonder why, sometimes, but you do. Did you know that when they got here, CJ and Nancy were arguing about the right kind of flour to use? I didn't even know CJ knew there were different kinds of flours. And that there are nine large coolers, nine of them, full of hot dogs and hamburgers for the kids to eat. Are there even that many kids in the entire town?"

"There are over two hundred children under the age of ten in the pack. Nancy and I put together a chart to see how a school would benefit the pack. And there are several different kinds of flours. But I believe they were talking about flowers, as in the type you plant. CJ is trying to get something to grow on the grounds in front of the house that will survive the children." She raised her head and looked at him. "Why do you love me?"

He smiled, and she felt better than she had in weeks. "Because I was fated to love you from birth, but more than that, because you love me, too. Because you put up with me. Because, and this is a biggy, you have nicer furniture than me."

She kissed him and pushed him back against the stash. When he lifted her off him, she felt her heart crack just a little. He grinned at her and pulled her to his body, where she could feel his cock.

"First, there was a coin in my ass and not in a good way. Also, Nancy gave me strict orders to have you back in one hour. She said that everyone is there to cheer you up and I was not to screw it up for them. I fear if I don't get you back on time, she'll send the pack for us. And as much as I'd like to take you on top of more money than I could spend in several lifetimes, she would beat me with that spoon of hers."

They were walking back hand in hand when they saw the families gathered together. She smiled at the picture they made, so many of them there for a single purpose: to make her happy. She looked at Myles.

"I would like to adopt Patrick. He's so adorable, and I very much would like to raise him as our own." The little boy seemed to know they were talking about him and turned to race toward them. "He doesn't have to be our only child, does he?"

"No. When we get everyone out of our house," Myles wiggled his brows at her, "we'll work on that right away."

CHAPTER 17

"They said not to be late. And we're going to be if you two don't get a move on." Myles grinned at her as he helped Patrick put his shoes on. "I thought you had those on already, young man."

"I got mud on them and you said not to get mud in the house again." Patrick looked at him, then at Chris. "You sure are cranky."

"I am not cranky. I'm reflective. There's difference." Chris walked away, and Myles winked at Patrick when he tied his shoe.

"She needs a nap." Patrick said as he ran out of the house. Myles was going to find his lovely wife. She was standing in the kitchen, stacking cookies on the platter. When she glared at him, he grinned.

"He wanted the blue one. And, of course, they were on the bottom. It is his birthday party." She nodded and walked to the door with her burden and he took it from her. "You should know that Patrick says you need a nap. Maybe later we can both take one. I bought a new toy to play with."

"You should stay off the internet is what you should do. How many toys have you bought so far? We haven't even told anyone that we're having a baby and you've spent a fortune on it." She opened the van door and slipped in and he put the tray of cookies in the back and got in the front.

"The toy isn't for the new one. It's for us." Myles grinned at her when she looked at him like a fish out of water, then she snapped her mouth closed so quickly that he was sure she had cracked her tooth. When she turned to him, he could see her red cheeks and the flush of desire on her skin. He told Patrick to close his eyes, he was going to kiss his mom, and the boy pretended to gag when Myles took her mouth.

He drove to the pack house, where everyone was waiting. They were late. He knew it was mostly his fault, but he was having so much fun working on the house and the yard. Myles got out and walked over to the men who were roasting a large hog while Chris and Patrick took his cookies into the house. The smells were enough to make a grown man whimper.

"You're late." Austin grinned at him. "We just got here too. Man, having two sets of twins is murder on a sex life."

Austin and CJ had just had another set of twins. These were boys. Myles watched as Holly walked by them with a baby in her arms, as well. She and Phil had two, one of each. The Force family was becoming very large.

"I heard that Gordon and Connor's wives are having a contest to see who pops first. My money in on Lou. Man, she is huge." Myles laughed when Dallas had lowered his voice to deliver the last comment.

Stacy held the hand of a little girl they had adopted last summer when he and Chris had adopted Patrick. Summer, he thought her name was, was a beautiful little thing and had finally grown into her hair. Myles had never seen such curls on one small child like she had.

Taking a beer from Connor he walked to where Chris was helping put the food out. She looked so happy he wanted to take her away and make love to her. She looked at him when he came up behind her and put his hand around her waist.

"Have you ever noticed how many babies are around here?" He nodded and told her that he'd been noticing the same thing. "Do you think that there'll be more?"

Nancy came out of the house with a child on her hip and holding the hand of another. He wasn't sure whose it was, but it didn't seem to matter to her who they belonged to. She loved them all.

"I think that Nancy would like that very much." She looked their way and handed off the children and came toward them. "I think we're about to get a lecture."

"I should beat you for not telling." Myles didn't comment, but Chris started to explain. He laughed when Nancy put her hand over her mouth.

"I was talking about the money from the sale of the paintings. You shouldn't have..." She brushed at a tear. "You're really going to have a baby?"

Chris nodded. "I'm not that far along. Just a few weeks. We were waiting to tell everyone. I didn't want to spoil the day for the kids."

"Oh that's just wonderful. Another grandbaby for me." Neither Myles nor Chris corrected her on her status as a grandmother. She had adopted them both as her children when they got married last fall.

"What is it you were going to beat me for?" Myles had wondered the same thing. As far as he knew they'd been too busy working to have done anything that would warrant a good beating.

"The money from the sale. I know you donated it all to the building of the new school. And you are wonderful to do so. I had no idea that the house and all its contents came to you when that horrible man died, but it has helped us here." Nancy hugged them both. "You two are going to make all of us so happy in a few weeks when you tell."

After she left, Chris turned to him. "You know anything about us getting that house? I know after we took everything of value out of it that they had declared it unfit for humans and I thought the council was taking it for past due something or another. I think it's a crock of shit, but there you have it."

"I'll see if I can corner Phil. He might know a bit about it. He's still working with you on the stuff in the tunnel as well at the stuff we moved?" She nodded. "He is a good man and trustworthy. He won't cheat anyone."

"I know that. But there are times when I think he's getting too much for some of it. Leon seems to think that most of the stuff in the house was stolen. I wish we could figure out how to return it to them." She looked around. "And the fact that he gave me that stupid crown makes me want to murder him in his sleep."

"Talking about me again, Chris dear." Myles laughed at Phil when he spoke up behind her and then at the look on Chris's face. He was going to pay dearly for that.

"Yes, I am. What is this Nancy says about the house being ours? I thought you said that Gates owed like millions of dollars in dues and they wanted it." Phil nodded and leaned against the table.

"It's yours because Leon gave it to you." Myles looked over at the man in question as he pushed three swings filled with children. "His name was on the deed and, as he didn't have a job, nor receive, any sort of monies when he worked for the vamp, he couldn't have been responsible for the master's debt. And the debt was Gates's."

"He owned the house." Phil shrugged at Chris's question. "Or you found a deed that had his name on it."

Phil stood up. "Something like that. He deserved whatever we could give him. The things he had to do, the people he had to… Were you aware that he is solely responsible for getting that pack of wolves that had been at the mansion calmed and trained enough to be donated to zoos around the world? No small feat for a man as old as him."

"How old is he?" Myles had wanted to ask Leon for months now. The man knew no bounds when it came to working, and he'd been so helpful around the yards, too.

"He is nearly as old as Gates was. My mother remembers him from when she was a child. And she said he was an adult then." Phil started away as he spoke over his shoulder. "If you're brave enough to ask mother how old she is, you'd add another thousand onto that. But I'd be careful when I asked. She is a little vain about it."

He and Chris looked at one another and laughed. He wasn't going ask her, and it appeared neither was Chris. They decided that he was older than them and left it at that.

~~~

Chris was tired but not exhausted. She walked out onto the deck while Myles gave Patrick his bath. They took turns doing it because he liked it that way. Patrick said that he could tell them how much he loved them better when he was alone with them. She liked it as well. It gave her special time with her son.

Leon walked up onto the deck a few minutes later and she smiled at him. He had been living with them until a few weeks before, and now he had his own home. They had yet to go and visit him.

"Mistress, I was wondering if I may have a word with you and his lordship." He cleared his throat. "I mean you and Myles."

They'd asked him to stop calling them "lady" and "lordship" but when he was nervous, like he seemed to be now, he would forget. She told him how Patrick was getting his bath and Myles would be down shortly.

"He had a lovely day for his party, did he not?" Chris agreed. "I so enjoyed myself, as well. I was able to learn a new game with Myles's brothers. I believe they called it 'pony shoes.'"

"Horse shoes. And I saw you playing. You seemed to be quite good at it." He nodded. "I'm glad you're here. I wanted to talk to you about the mansion. Phil told me today that you signed it over to us. You should keep it. Maybe sell it."

"Phil said the same, but he also cautioned me that it was a white elephant and that there would be few who could afford such a monstrosity. He said I would be better off donating it to someone and taking the tax break." Leon grinned at her. "He made me look up the words and phrases I did not understand."

Leon had gotten a computer and had been looking up all sorts of things. His favorite site was one called "Urban Dictionary." Leon was becoming quite the slang user. She laughed when he told her what each of the phrases had meant when he looked them up. Myles came out in the middle of one.

"You've been busy again. Good. Education is great, and you can't ever learn enough." He sat down next to her and wrapped his arm over her shoulder. "How are you, Leon? You ready to have a housewarming party at your new digs?"

Leon sat there for several seconds and then reached into his pocket and pulled out a small notebook. After scribbling in it for a minute or two, he put it back and smiled at Myles.

"I shall have to get back to you on that. But I have come here for educational purposes. I have an idea that I would enjoy putting past you." He pulled out a large envelope from the inside of his shirt. "I should like to have a library."

At first Chris thought he meant one in his home. And that this was a list of books he'd like. But when they opened the envelope there were drawings and plans for a new building. He wanted to have a library built.

"The plans were on the internet. I have made notes in the margins on changes I would like to see. The bottom floor would be for the children. The top for the parents and other adults." She started to read his notes as he continued. "I think it would be a place that would be, I believe the term is 'user friendly.' Computers and other things to learn from at each station in it."

"This is huge, Leon. Doable but a huge project." Myles looked up at him with a smile. "I thought you said you thought it was time to move on to explore."

Leon nodded. "I cannot think of a better way to explore than with children. They have such a wildly wonderful imagination. And they so enjoy telling you what they have discovered. I wish to explore the world through their eyes. With the new baby that you are now carrying."

Chris put her hand on her flat belly and looked up at him. His smile told her so much yet so very little. She had a feeling that he'd known since conception but didn't ask. She did however ask him if he knew the sex.

"Yes, Miss. It is a boy. He will be much like his father. Strong of mind and body. He will be intelligent beyond his years and show compassion to everyone he meets. But he will be ferocious with his enemies. Fair, but firm with everyone. He will be a great man among his people, as will all your children."

Chris nodded, not sure she could speak around the large lump in her throat. Myles thanked him and asked him about the building. She was sure it was to give her a few moments to gather herself.

"The funding will come from donations. I was not paid for working for the master, but I was through the agency. So I have very little of my own, though I do not need overly much. And Phil has assured me that I would be able to get donations from people in the pack as well as the vampires. He seems to think that it will be no problem to get it started." He handed them another envelope that he pulled from his shirt. "That is what he said I would need. I'm not sure if that is a great sum to you, but it is tremendous to me."

Myles laughed. "It's a great sum to anyone. But it's doable as well. I think this is a great plan, Leon, and better because you'll be hanging around with us a lot longer."

He left about an hour later, saying that he had some things he needed to look up. He was forever making notes and coming back with an answer to them. He and Patrick spent hour's daily going over things they found on the computer.

"He'll make this work, you know. I think that with very little effort, too." She nodded at Myles. "I'm guessing he'll have more than enough donations, too."

"You know he will. There isn't a person or family on this property that he hasn't helped in some way." She smiled. "And, of course, we do have all that extra gold we can help him with, too."

"I love you, Chris." She looked at her husband and smiled. "I mean really love you. You're the kindest, sweetest person I know. You wouldn't deny your husband or son anything."

She looked at him suspiciously. "What have you promised him now? Or better yet, what has he talked you into wanting to give him. You do realize that you're his dad and he's the child. You can tell him no."

"Like you do?" He grinned. "No, this is a wonderful idea. He wants to go on a trip. He says that in school they were learning about the great pyramids and he wants to see them in person. He said that, and I quote, 'they might blow away next month,' and where will he be with being the only little boy who's not seen them."

He had said something similar to her last night only it was a theme park he'd seen on television. Only that time it was the ocean taking it under. The boy was too smart for his own good.

"Have you seen them?" Myles shook his head. "I have. You do know that it's hot and sandy, right?"

"Yes, and you want to go as badly as I do, so forget about trying to make it sound like a hardship on you. And I know that we'll be going to Florida on our way, too. The travel agent called and said the tickets were on their way."

As they went up to bed, she touched some of the things that had been brought from the tunnels. A painting hung over the mantel, a large urn sat on the fireplace hearth. She had fallen in love with some of the coins, their age and value secondary to their workmanship and quality.

"We're going to need a bigger house." She looked at Myles. "If what Leon is saying is true, and I've no doubt that it is, we're going to need a bigger house."

"I would like that. Lots of children, ours and ones that need us." She had been meaning to talk to him about adopting more and this seemed the perfect time. "We could move into the mansion. After considerable work is done to it."

"I like that idea." He moved up the stairs behind her and held her to him. "I'm thinking that Leon has already started on it. He told me today that most of the furniture has been taken out and sold. And the upper levels have been completely cleaned and carpets replaced. He said that most of the money came from the cash he'd found after everyone had left. Plus, his house is on that property."

Chris laughed. She wished now that she'd hugged Leon harder. "He's going to keep going one step ahead of us daily if we don't want to stop him. I'm thinking we'll let him have his way a bit more before we reel him in."

Myles laughed, too, and they walked into their room. In the middle of the bed was Patrick and he was snoring softly. He was spread out like he was king of their bed.

"Want me to take him back to his room?" She shook her head. "Good. I love waking up next to him in the morning. Especially when he has his butt in my face."

Laughing, she dressed in her night clothes and climbed into bed with her two favorite men. Myles adjusted Patrick around so that he wasn't taking up the entire bed and growled softly when he moved right back. Things were never going to be boring in this household.

ABOUT THE AUTHOR

Kathi Barton, author of the bestselling series Force of Nature, lives in Nashport, Ohio with her husband Paul. In addition to writing full time Kathi likes to spend time with her eight grandkids, three children and three children-in-laws. She writes to relax and have fun.

Her muse, a cross between Jimmy Stewart and Hugh Jackman brings them to life for her readers in a way that has them coming back time and again for more. Her favorite genre is paranormal romance with a great deal of spice. You can visit Kathi on line and drop her an email if you'd like. She loves hearing from her fans. aaronskiss@gmail.com.

Follow Kathi on her blog:
http://kathisbartonauthor.blogspot.com/